A Kiss in Rome

G·K
·Hall
&Co.

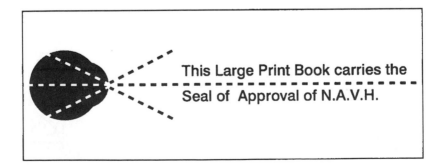

A Kiss in Rome

Barbara Cartland

G.K. Hall & Co • Thorndike, Maine

Published in 2001 by arrangement with
International Book Marketing Limited.

G.K. Hall Large Print Paperback Series.

The text of this Large Print edition is unabridged.
Other aspects of the book may vary from the original edition.

Set in 16 pt. Plantin by Al Chase.

Printed in the United States on permanent paper.

Library of Congress Cataloging-in-Publication Data
Cartland, Barbara, 1902–
    A kiss in Rome / Barbara Cartland.
        p.   cm.
    ISBN 0-7838-9442-2 (lg. print : sc : alk. paper)
    1. British — Italy — Fiction.   2. Rome (Italy) — Fiction.
3. Large type books.   I. Title.
PR6005.A765 K54 2001
823′.912—dc21   2001016740

author's note

The first time I visited Rome I was entranced by the beauty of its treasures and the history which one finds at every turn.

It is undoubtedly one of the most beautiful Cities in the world and every stone appears to have a story attached to it.

The Villa Borghese, which I have described in this novel and which in the past was called a Palace, is one of the jewels of Europe.

It is breath-taking in the beauty of its rooms and their contents.

It was built originally by Cardinal Camillo Borghese in 1605 when he came to the Papal throne, taking the name Paul V.

The treasures were added to year by year with each generation.

But it makes one's heart sink to learn that the famous collection of antique sculpture to which had been added the Masterpieces of Bernini, making in all 523 pieces, was given by Camillo Borghese, the husband of the beautiful Pauline Bonaparte, to his brother-in-law Napoleon in 1807 and was carried off bodily to Paris.

This is typical of conquerors all down the ages.

Fortunately, however, most of these were returned eventually to Rome, where we may still see them.

The exquisite statue of Pauline Borghese, who was the second wife of Prince Camillo Borghese, is the masterpiece of Antonio Canova (1757–1822).

It is now on show in one of the rooms and was sculpted in 1805.

It shows Pauline semi-nude, reclining on a divan, half raised up and holding in her left hand the apple of victory won — as Venus — for her beauty.

I have written another novel which includes the Borghese Palace, called *The Coin of Love*.

In this novel, which I wrote after my visit in 1988, I have described the magic of the Trevi Fountain and the glory of the Colosseum.

But one has only to arrive in Rome and visit a list of the places that move one and excite the imagination to find there are hundreds more waiting for one's appreciation.

Rome is known as the "Eternal City" and as long as its treasures remain it will always have a place in the hearts of those who love beauty.

chapter one

Alina Langley looked around the room and wondered miserably if there was anything left to sell.

Everything that was of any real value had already gone.

The patches on the wall where the mirrors had hung and the gap where the pretty inlaid *secrétaire* had stood made her want to cry.

"What can I do?" she asked. "What can I do?"

It seemed incredible that everything had happened so quickly.

From feeling safe and happy in the world around her, she now felt as if the ceiling had crashed down on her head.

When her Father a year ago had had a fall out hunting and broken his spine, it was for her Mother as if the world had come to an end.

They had been extremely happy together.

They were not rich, but had enough money to enjoy their horses and the few acres of land by which they were surrounded.

Then, when Sir Oswald died, it was found that he had run up a mountain of debts.

They were certainly not due to riotous living.

He had not paid his taxes and he owed a great deal to his Coach-Builder and to the builders for repairs to the house.

What was worse, shares in Companies in which he had invested both his wife's and his own money had proved worthless.

Lady Langley, however, was not the slightest perturbed by this.

She only knew that without her husband she had no wish to go on living.

To Alina it was horrifying to see her Mother fading away.

She was still so young and beautiful and had always seemed like a girl.

As she had no wish to live, Lady Langley simply died so that she could be with her husband again.

It was then that Alina knew she was alone in the world and, what was even more frightening, that she had no money.

The house was hers because she was an only child, but how could she keep it up?

Anything that was valuable had been sold off to pay her Father's debts.

A few other things which she cherished she had had to sell to pay for special food and medicines for her Mother.

It was just a waste of money, for Lady Langley never got better, and had never intended to do so.

Alina walked to the window to look out at the garden.

The daffodils made a golden patch of colour beneath the trees.

The almond trees were just coming into

bloom, and the grass was growing on the lawns.

The sun was shining and she opened the window.

She could hear the song of the birds and the buzz of the bees hovering over the blossom.

It was so familiar.

She felt as if they were telling her that they sympathised with her in her predicament and how they wished they could help.

"What can I do?" she asked the wrens who were watching her from a bush that was just beginning to show the green leaves of Spring.

It was then, to her surprise, that she heard in the distance wheels approaching the front-door.

She wondered who it could be.

The only people who had called on her after her Mother's Funeral had been from the village, and they had walked.

She thought it might be the Doctor, who had always been a friend.

Then she remembered that he had gone away, on a short holiday.

Slowly, because she almost resented being disturbed in her loneliness, she walked from the Drawing-Room out into the Hall.

The woman who came to clean in the morning had already left and she opened the door herself.

A very smart carriage was standing outside.

There was a face at its window that made her cry out in astonishment.

"Denise! Is it really you?"

She ran down the steps, and as the elegantly

dressed figure got out of the carriage, she flung her arms around her.

"Denise, how wonderful to see you!" she exclaimed. "I thought you had forgotten all about me."

"No, of course not," Denise Sedgwick replied, "but I have come to ask for your help."

"My help?" Alina repeated in surprise.

She could not imagine how Denise Sedgwick could possibly want her help.

Her Mother had been a distant Cousin of the Sedgwicks and had been devoted to Denise's Mother before she had died in childbirth.

Because Alina and Denise were almost the same age, with Denise just a few months older, it was arranged that they should take lessons together.

Every Monday Alina would ride over to the large house, which was only three miles away across the fields, and stay there until Friday.

On Friday she returned home to be with her Father and Mother.

It had been a very satisfactory arrangement from Lady Langley's point of view.

Because Denise's Father was wealthy, he could afford the best-educated Governesses.

They also had a number of Tutors for various additional subjects in which he wanted his daughter to be educated.

Alina enjoyed her lessons and loved being with Denise.

She was very lovely; in fact, both girls were

outstandingly beautiful.

Perhaps Denise was the more sensational of the two, having perfect features and chestnut hair that was tipped with little flames of red.

Her eyes were the green of a forest stream.

It was no surprise when, just before her eighteenth birthday, Denise went to London to be presented at Court by her Grandmother.

She had been an outstanding success.

In fact, she was such a sensation that Alina lost touch with her.

At first the two girls had corresponded frequently.

But soon Alina found that she was writing three letters to one hurried note from Denise.

She therefore thought that perhaps she was imposing on their friendship and wrote only occasionally.

Lately she had not written at all.

Now Denise was saying:

"Dearest, you must forgive me for not having come to see you sooner. I have not been at home or with my Grandmother, but staying in all sorts of exciting houses, for house-parties which I am longing to tell you about."

"You look lovely!" Alina exclaimed.

She was looking, as she spoke, at the very elegant travelling-coat which Denise was wearing, and at her hat trimmed with feathers.

She noted too the elegance of her gloves, her shoes, and her hand-bag — in fact, everything about her.

They went into the Drawing-Room and Denise gave a cry of surprise.

"What has happened?" she exclaimed. "What have you done? Where are all the mirrors and the pictures?"

"I have a lot to tell you," Alina said quietly.

Denise waited and Alina went on:

"After Papa died we found we were very poor."

"I was so upset to hear about his accident," Denise murmured sympathetically. "But I had always imagined you were very comfortably off."

"We thought we were," Alina replied, "but there were a great many debts, and Papa's investments did not pay any dividends."

Denise clasped her hands together.

"Oh, dearest, how terrible! I wish I had known. Of course I would have wanted to help you."

Alina drew in her breath.

"I do not think you know," she said, "that Mama . . . died three weeks ago."

Denise gave a little cry of horror and flung her arms round Alina.

"I had no idea — oh, Alina, I am so sorry! I know how much you loved her, and I loved her too."

"Everybody loved Mama," Alina said, "but she could not go on living without Papa."

Denise sat down on a sofa that needed repairing.

"You must tell me all about it," she said. "I had no idea that anything like this had happened. When I decided to come to you for help, I expected, of course, to find your Mother here with everything as beautiful as I remembered it to be."

"We had to sell everything that was saleable," Alina said in a low voice.

There was a little pause before she added:

"We will talk about that later. I want to hear about you and the success you have been, and, of course, why you have come to me for help."

She saw by the expression in her friend's eyes that something was really wrong.

After a moment Denise said:

"Oh, Alina, I have been such a fool! You will not believe how stupid I have been."

Alina sat down beside her.

"Tell me about it."

"That is what I decided to do and why I came," Denise replied, "and I was sure you would help me."

Alina reached out and took Denise's hand in hers.

"Start at the beginning," she said.

"Well, as you heard, I was a success in London. I really was a great success, Alina, and it would be stupid to deny it."

"How could you be anything else?" Alina asked fondly. "You are so lovely and you have all those beautiful clothes that you wrote and told me about."

"My Grandmother was very generous," Denise said, "and, of course, Papa was prepared to pay for anything I wanted."

There was a smile on her lips as she added:

"I really was the Belle of every Ball I went to!"

"Of course you were!" Alina said loyally.

"It is not only looks that count in London," Denise said. "There are plenty of sophisticated Beauties who fascinate the Prince of Wales and all the smart gentlemen who frequent Marlborough House."

"I am sure none of them could be as beautiful as you!" Alina said.

"They think they are far more beautiful, and the men who go after them are not interested in *débutantes*."

Alina waited, wondering what was wrong.

"However, I have had dozens of proposals," Denise said, "and finally, Alina, I lost my heart!"

"How exciting!" Alina exclaimed. "Who is he? And are you very happy?"

Denise gave a deep sigh.

"He is very handsome and he is the Earl of Wescott, so Papa was only too delighted at the idea of my marrying him."

"You are going to be married?" Alina exclaimed.

"That is what has gone wrong," Denise answered.

"But what has happened?"

"I cannot understand how I can have been such a fool!" Denise said. "Henry was in love with me, very much in love with me, and asked me to marry him."

Alina was listening wide-eyed.

She could not understand what she was hearing.

"I do not know what came over me," Denise continued, "but I think it was because Henry rather took it for granted that I would accept him. Although there could be no question of my doing anything else, I prevaricated."

"You mean," Alina said, "that you did not accept him."

"I did — in a way — but told him he would have to wait a little for us to be quite certain that we really loved each other."

"And he disagreed?"

"No. But, Alina, I was so stupid! Just to make him more in love with me and a little jealous, I flirted with a lot of other men, until finally I went too far."

"What happened then?" Alina asked.

"Henry wrote me a letter saying it was quite obvious that I did not really care for him, and he left England!"

There was a note of despair in Denise's voice which Alina did not miss.

"He left England?" she questioned. "But where has he gone?"

"He has gone to Rome to stay with his Grand-mother," Denise replied, "and I am terrified — yes, terrified — that I shall never see him again."

"But, surely, if you write to him . . ." Alina began.

"I am not going to do that," Denise said. "I

have decided to go to Rome and see him. I know when he sees me again, everything will be all right. I can tell him that I love him more than anything on earth, and we will be married."

Alina thought for a moment before she said:

"I am sure that is a sensible solution."

"But it will be difficult," Denise said, "and that is why I have come to see you."

"What can I do?" Alina asked.

"Well, Papa has agreed that I can go to Rome, and, as it happens, my Cousin, Lord Teverton, whom you have never met, is going there on a special mission on behalf of the Prime Minister. I can travel with him, but, of course, I have to have a chaperon."

Alina nodded.

She could understand that it would be impossible for a young girl to go abroad without one.

"That is why I came to see you," Denise said, "because I have been trying to remember the name of that Governess we had for a short while when Miss Smithson was ill. She was a married woman, and a very pleasant lady."

"A Governess?" Alina repeated. "But, surely . . . ?"

"I know what you are thinking," Denise said, "exactly the same as Papa did, that I should take one of my relatives with me. An Aunt, or an elder Cousin."

She threw out her hands in a very expressive gesture.

"Can you imagine what they would be like?

They would be coy and say 'Now, you young people want to be alone together,' which would make me feel hot with embarrassment. Or else they will play the strict chaperon and never allow me to be alone with Henry for an instant."

Alina laughed.

She had met some of Denise's relatives and knew that was exactly the way they would behave.

"I went over a whole list of them," Denise was saying, "and each one seemed worse than the last. I have to be very clever with Henry, as I have really upset him."

She made a sound that was almost a sob as she said:

"His letter was such a shock to me. I know he has taken umbrage at the way I behaved, and I have somehow to make him forgive me."

She sighed again, then with a little flash in her eyes she added:

"But I am not going to crawl at his feet, which would be very bad for his ego. He is quite authoritative enough as it is!"

Alina laughed again.

"I can see your problem, but Mrs. Wilson, which is the name of the lady about whom you were asking, is working for the French Ambassador, teaching his children to speak English. At the moment she is with them in France."

"Oh, bother!" Denise said. "She was the only person I could think of who could be tactful and at the same time satisfy Papa that she was the right sort of chaperon for me."

"I am sure you can think of somebody else," Alina said hopefully.

"I simply cannot think who —" Denise began.

Then she gave a sudden scream.

It was so loud that it made Alina start, and she looked at her friend in surprise.

"But of course — I have solved the problem!" Denise said. "It is quite easy. You will come with me!"

"Me?" Alina asked. "But, dearest, I am not a married woman, and two girls together could not chaperon each other."

"Of course I understand that," Denise said sharply. "What I am thinking of, and it is really clever of me, is that you should come as your Mother."

"M-my . . . Mother?"

"You know how lovely your Mother was and how young she looked," Denise said, thinking it out in her mind. "After all, we all know the story of how she married when she was seventeen, so she cannot have been quite thirty-seven when she died."

"That is true," Alina said, "but —"

"There are no 'buts,' " Denise interrupted. "I shall tell Papa, who is leaving this afternoon for a week's racing at Doncaster, that Lady Langley is chaperoning me to Rome. In fact, when I left the house he said:

" 'Remember me to Lady Langley. She was always a very charming woman and I am sorry we have not seen more of her.' He has obviously not heard of her death."

Alina was staring at her friend as if she could not believe what she was hearing.

Then, as Denise stopped speaking, she said:

"It is a wonderful idea, darling, and you know I would adore to come with you to Rome, but no-one in their senses would believe I was Mama . . . even if I dressed up in her clothes."

"Why not?" Denise argued obstinately. "People used to say that you and your Mother looked more like sisters. If you did your hair in a more sophisticated style and wore a little powder and rouge as the Beauties do in London, I am sure you would look a lot older."

Alina did not speak, and after a moment Denise continued:

"I remember all the flattering praise you used to get at the Christmas parties when we put on those Charades and Plays for Papa's guests. I used to be jealous because they always said you were a much better actress than I was."

She put her fingers up to her forehead in thought.

Then she added:

"You remember the Restoration Play we put on the Christmas before I went to London? You played two parts in it: one was a very sophisticated and witty woman who was supposed to be at least forty."

"Acting on a stage is one thing," Alina said, "but if I was doing it at close quarters, I am quite certain no-one would be deceived."

Denise threw out her hands.

"Who is there to be deceived?" she asked. "Papa will have left for the Races. My Cousin, Lord Teverton, has never met you, nor has my lady's-maid and the Courier who will be escorting us."

Alina did not speak, and she went on:

"When we get to Rome, all I want you to do is to let me see Henry alone, and I am sure you can amuse yourself by looking at the Colosseum and all those other places about which we used to read with Miss Smithson."

There was a sudden light in Alina's eyes.

She was thinking of how much she had longed to see all the places they had read about.

She often thought about them when she was alone at night.

She pretended she was actually seeing them with her eyes instead of just remembering what she had read.

Then she told herself she had to be firm about this.

"Dearest Denise," she said at length. "You know I would do anything to help you — anything in the world — except something which is wrong and might cause trouble for you, one way or another."

"What you can do for me is quite simple," Denise answered. "You will come with me to Rome as my chaperon, and you will make quite certain that Henry Wescott forgives me and we become officially engaged."

Alina thought it all sounded too easy to be true.

Then she said in a frightened voice:

"Y-you are quite certain I would not . . . make a mess of it?"

"Why should you?" Denise enquired. "We will not see anyone who has ever seen your Mother, and you have to admit that she did look very young."

"Yes . . . Everyone said so," Alina agreed.

"Then all you have to do is to make yourself look a little older than you are now. Good gracious! If you cannot act the part of a Lady who is a suitable chaperon for me, what can you do?"

Alina laughed.

"You are being ridiculous! At the same time, you know, dearest, because I do want to help you and also because, if I am honest, I would love to go to Rome, I am longing to say 'Yes.' "

"That is wonderful!" Denise cried. "We leave in three days' time."

"Three . . . days?" Alina repeated.

"That will be plenty of time for you to decide which of your Mother's clothes you are going to wear, and I will provide you with everything else."

She put her hand over Alina's as she said:

"I am so ashamed of myself for not realising before now how poor you are. I have mountains of clothes, really mountains of them, which I could have sent you, but I was so selfish I did not think of it."

"You are not to blame yourself," Alina said, "and what would I do with mountains of clothes in Little Benbury?"

"You can wear them," Denise answered, "but the gown you have on now is a disaster!"

"I have had it for years," Alina admitted, "and it is rather threadbare."

"Throw it away — throw everything you have away, and I am sure there are furs and jewels that belonged to my Mother of the kind you would be expected to wear."

Alina looked at her questioningly, and Denise said:

"Now, let us work this out carefully. You are not coming as the country-bred and impoverished Lady Langley who is chaperoning me because Papa is paying her to do so."

Alina made a little sound and she went on:

"I will of course pay you myself. I have an absolute mint of money! But you will have to look rich and a Lady of Fashion, or people will not be impressed by you."

"Why do you want them to be impressed?" Alina asked.

"I want Henry to be impressed, for one," Denise said. "I have no wish for him to think I am just running after him. I have got to arrive in Rome with a different reason for going there, and that could be that I am accompanying Lady Langley, who is a friend of my family, because she has recently been widowed and is feeling lonely."

"You are making a whole drama out of it," Alina protested.

"That is what I intend to do," Denise said. "And I will write your part just as you used to write one for me in the past. Now I will do it for you."

Alina laughed.

"Oh, Denise, you are incorrigible!" she said. "But I am sure you are making a terrible mistake. There must be plenty of people more suitable than I am to go with you to Rome. Suppose I make mistakes and give the show away?"

"I have never known you to fail at anything," Denise said. "You are much cleverer than I am. Every one of my Governesses, Tutors, or anyone else who taught us always used to say:

" 'Now, come along, Miss Denise, try and be as clever as your Cousin who, after all, is younger than you!' "

Denise was mimicking a Tutor's voice, and Alina threw her arms round her neck and kissed her.

"Oh, Denise, it is such Heaven being with you again," she said. "I have missed you so much and all the things we used to laugh about together."

"That is what we are going to do all the way to Rome. Otherwise I shall just sit here and mope," Denise answered. "You have to keep me laughing and sparkling so that when Henry sees me he realises what a mistake he made in leaving me."

"I cannot think why he should have done so, seeing how beautiful you are," Alina said.

"It was my own fault," Denise said in a low voice, "and if I lose him, Alina, it would break my heart. I could never love anyone else in the same way."

She was speaking in a very different tone of voice. Then she reached out and took her Cousin's hand.

"Help me . . . please . . . help me!" she begged. "I know my whole happiness is at stake. If I lose Henry, nothing else will ever be the same again."

There was a cry in her voice that tore at Alina's heart.

She knew she would do anything, however difficult, if it would help Denise.

"I will come," she said, "but you will have to tell me exactly how I should behave. Remember, I have never been to London or seen any of the smart, sophisticated women I am to impersonate."

"They are all very much alike," Denise answered. "They behave as if the world were made for them to walk on and believe that every man at whom they smile is very lucky and should feel as if he has just won a million pounds on the Race-Course."

Alina giggled.

"Can you see me behaving like that?"

"Of course I can," Denise said, "and that is exactly what you have to do. You are very grand, very self-important, and very rich!"

"I would certainly need to be a good actress to make them believe that!" Alina remarked.

"Why did you not tell me?" Denise asked. "I cannot bear to think of your selling all the lovely things in this room."

"I was just wondering before you arrived what else I could possibly sell, or how I could work to earn some money."

"You have got it," Denise replied. "You are going to work for me and I am prepared to pay you anything you ask."

She put her arms round Alina as she spoke and kissed her.

"I love you, Alina," she said, "and we shall have a marvellous time together. When I am married to Henry, I will find you a husband who is just as rich as he is!"

"I shall be quite content for the moment just to see the Colosseum and St. Peter's," Alina said.

"From what I have been told," Denise answered, "Rome is packed with marvellous treasures of every sort. So if you are prepared to go sight-seeing, you will be able to do so from morning to night."

"That is all I want," Alina said, "and I shall certainly not interfere with you and the Earl."

There was a pause before Denise said with almost a sob:

"Oh, Alina . . . do you think he has . . . forgotten me already? Supposing he has found an . . . Italian girl who is more . . . beautiful than I am?"

"I do not believe it possible," Alina answered, "and if he has, it means that he is not really in love with you. You know we always used to say when we were younger that what we wanted to find was real love, which means we have found the other half of ourselves."

"That is true," Denise said. "Do you re-member Miss Smithson saying the Ancient Greeks believed that after God had made man and thought he wanted a companion, He cut him in half and called the soft, gentle, sweet part of him woman?"

"I remember her saying that," Alina said, "and what we are searching for is the other half of our-selves."

"Of course," Denise agreed, "and that is what Henry is to me — I know he is!"

"How could you have been unkind to him?" Alina asked. "He must have been very unhappy to have rushed away from you in that abrupt manner."

"Do not talk about it," Denise begged. "I was a fool — I know I was a fool! I just wanted to make him a little jealous so that he would be more in love with me than he was already. But I . . . went too . . . far!"

Alina put her arm around her friend's shoul-ders.

"Do not worry, dearest," she said. "I am sure

you will be able to get him back, and I will pray very hard that he is as miserable without you as you are without him."

"I remember your prayers," Denise said. "You always said they were answered."

"That is what I am thinking of at this moment. When I pray for a solution to my own problems, I even ask the birds outside for help!"

"And here I am, ready to help you," Denise replied. "Now, let us make plans."

Because she was so determined to take Alina with her to Rome, Denise worked it out very intelligently.

First of all, as her Father was going away immediately, she thought it would be possible for Alina to come to Sedgwick House, her own home.

Then they thought that the servants would know her and that could be dangerous.

"I will pick you up here on Wednesday morning," Denise decided, "and we will drive to the train together. When we reach London, Lord Teverton will be waiting for us at his house in Belgrave Square."

"I have no idea what he is like," Alina said. "Supposing he is suspicious?"

"You need not worry about him," Denise said. "He is extremely angry that I am to travel with him to Rome, so I doubt if he will so much as speak to us."

Alina looked surprised.

"Why not?" she asked.

"Because he is stuck up and interested only in

himself!" Denise said. "He is a huge success in London and a close friend of the Prince of Wales."

She lowered her voice, almost as if she were afraid she would be overheard.

"He also has affairs with the great Beauties, and I am told that when he leaves them, they cry their eyes out!"

Alina did not understand.

"Leaves them?"

"You know what I mean," Denise said.

She saw that her Cousin was looking perplexed and explained:

"He has what are called *affaires de coeur*, and because he is so smart and also so rich, the women run after him as if he were a golden apple at the top of a pear tree!"

Alina laughed.

"I do not believe it!"

"It is true!" Denise said. "He gives himself frightful airs and behaves as if everybody is beneath his condescension."

"He sounds horrible!" Alina said.

"I have disliked him for years," Denise replied. "He always speaks to me as if I were a mentally deficient child!"

"I cannot believe this!"

"It is true, and it is only because he enjoys riding my Father's horses that he comes to stay with us at all. And, of course, they meet on the Race-Course."

She gave a little laugh before she said:

"I saw his face when Papa asked him to take me with him to Rome."

"He was not pleased at the idea?" Alina said.

"He was horrified!" Denise answered. "I could see him thinking up a dozen different excuses for refusing. Then finally, very grudgingly, he accepted the responsibility of having me with him, providing I had a chaperon."

Alina thought indignantly that it was incredible that anyone could be unkind to someone as pretty and sweet as Denise.

She remembered her Father once saying that the young men in London thought *débutantes* were a bore.

Therefore, the sooner they were married off to a suitable husband, the better.

"Why has your Cousin never married?" she asked now. "How old is he?"

"All of thirty," Denise replied, "and he can hardly marry any of the women to whom he makes love because they are always already married."

Alina's eyes widened.

"Surely their husbands object?"

"They do not know about it. You would be amazed at how extraordinarily women behave in London. The Prince of Wales always associates with married women who are beautiful, witty, and very sophisticated. My Cousin, Marcus Teverton, behaves in the same way."

"Well, I think it is horrid!" Alina said firmly. "I cannot imagine Papa would have behaved like that, and, if he had, it would have broken Mama's heart."

"Your Father and Mother were so different from anybody else," Denise said. "I never thought of her dying. She always seemed so young and happy."

"She was until she lost Papa," Alina said softly, "but then the light went out, and she could not bear to be in the darkness alone."

There was a break in her voice as she spoke.

It was still hard to speak of her Mother without the tears coming into her eyes.

"Poor Alina!" Denise said. "I know how much you must miss her. It would be the best thing in the world for you to come to Rome, and I am sure it is what she would want you to do."

Alina hesitated.

"Perhaps Mama would be shocked at the idea of my telling lies and playing a part that is deceitful."

"If you ask me," Denise said, "I think she would consider it a great joke. You know how she used to laugh at the 'fuddy-duddy' people in the County who disapproved of everything we did."

She saw Alina was looking a little happier and went on:

"Do you remember when they said the hedges we jumped were too high for us, and we acted like young hooligans? It was your Mother who said she thought it was a very good thing for women to be able to ride well and not be afraid of a high jump."

Alina nodded.

"That is what we are going to do now," Denise continued. "We are going to take a high jump and you will forget all your problems. You will see Rome and all the beautiful things it contains."

Alina gave a little cry.

"Do you really think, Denise, that I can do it? I want to, and it will be a great adventure!"

"Of course it will," Denise agreed, "and I will supply the happy ending when I marry Henry and make sure he never leaves me again."

"Oh, dearest," Alina said, "I do want you to be happy."

chapter two

Denise arrived the next afternoon.

Alina watched in astonishment as the coachman and footman carried in a number of trunks.

They put them in Alina's bed-room and as soon as they had done so Denise started to open them.

"I have brought you Mama's luggage," she said. "It has her initials on it and looks, I am sure, much more luxurious than anything you have."

Alina was aware of that and she also saw the initials "A.L." on the trunks.

Before she could ask the question, Denise said:

"You must remember that Mama's name was Alice."

"Of course it was!" Alina exclaimed. "I had forgotten."

"I suddenly thought of the luggage when I was driving home," Denise said with glee. "As soon as I told Papa that Lady Langley was chaperoning me — and he was delighted about it — I went upstairs to the attics. All Mama's things were there — and look what I found!"

She opened the trunks one by one.

First she lifted out an evening-cloak of black

velvet trimmed with ermine.

Alina made a little murmur of delight.

Denise then produced another cloak which was of blue velvet trimmed with Russian sables.

"They are lovely!" Alina exclaimed.

"Wait!" Denise said.

She then produced a sable stole with lots of tails.

Alina knew most Ladies of Fashion wore this type of fur if they could afford it.

There was also a number of sunshades which were very elegant.

Then Denise opened a large hat-box.

"I thought Mama's other clothes were far too out of date for you to wear them," she said, "except for a few evening-gowns. But hats have altered very little since she died; in fact, they are now only more elaborate."

She removed a number of hats trimmed with feathers and bows of ribbon.

Alina realised they would make her look older.

She could also take the decoration from one hat to make another look more spectacular.

"You know how elaborate everything is to-day," Denise was saying, "and that is why I am sure we can add lace and frills to the evening-gowns so that they look up-to-date."

The bustle, which had been very prominent when Denise's Mother was alive, had gradually become more a part of the skirt.

But for older women the evening-gowns with

their trains were still very much the same as they had been.

"I am sure we can find a Dressmaker in Rome who can smarten up some of these gowns," Denise said. "In the meantime, I have brought you every gown of mine that does not look obviously as if it belonged to a *débutante*."

There were a great number of them, and Denise unpacked them quickly, saying:

"I always thought that one unbecoming because it was too dark, and this one I bought in a bad light. I really think it would become you, while on me it is a disaster."

Certainly the darker dresses with their rich colours threw into prominence Alina's very fair hair and the whiteness of her skin.

Finally Denise brought a small box from the last trunk with an air of triumph.

"Look what I found also in the attic!" she said.

She opened the box and Alina saw that inside there was face-powder, mascara, and a tiny pot of rouge.

"How could your Mother have had that?" she asked.

"That is a question that worried me," Denise replied, "until I remembered one of our Cousins who was very smart and very sophisticated coming to stay. I could not have been very old at the time, but I can remember her laughing at Mama and saying she was 'old-fashioned.' After she left, a small parcel arrived which was a present from her."

" 'What do you think Gwen has sent me?' I heard my Mother ask Papa.

" 'I have no idea,' he replied.

"She opened the box and showed him what was inside," Denise went on.

"And what did your Father say?" Alina enquired.

"I remember him roaring in fury:

" 'I am not having my wife looking like an actress!'

"My Mother laughed at him.

" 'If we go to London,' she said, 'you will be ashamed of me for looking so countrified.'

" 'That is how I like you,' Papa replied, and put his arms round her.

"So she never used it," Denise finished, "but now you will find it very useful."

"But . . . I have no wish to look like an actress!" Alina protested.

"Gwen sent Mama the present ten years ago," Denise said. "Since then things have changed. All the smart women in London use a little powder, a touch of rouge, and their lips are always invitingly pink."

Alina laughed.

"Well, I shall be inviting nobody, but if you want me to look the part, I suppose I shall have to accept the 'stage props.' "

"Of course you must," Denise insisted.

She did not stay long but hurried away, leaving Alina to put all the clothes she had brought back into the trunks.

She added some clothes that had belonged to her Mother.

Lady Langley had always been elegantly dressed, even though she could not spend a lot of money on her clothes.

But they were certainly very much smarter than anything Alina now owned.

She therefore left her own dress hanging in the wardrobe.

She found, which had belonged to her Mother, a very pretty travelling-gown in a deep blue satin.

It was fortunate that it could go under a cloak which Denise had brought her of almost the same shade of blue.

It was trimmed with just a little fur, which made it not look too smart for a journey.

There was a hat which Alina thought was really very becoming.

She added a few small feathers and a velvet bow to the crown.

Among the sunshades there was a hand-bag.

"I am afraid there is only one of those," Denise had said as she took it out of the box. "But Papa gave a lot of Mama's belongings away to her relations after she died. They all asked for hand-bags because they knew the ones Mama possessed all came from a very expensive shop in Bond Street."

"I am delighted to have that one," Alina said. "I am afraid that if anyone saw the bag I have been using, they would not for a moment believe

I was rich enough to have any money inside it."

"Then throw it away," Denise said, "because that is the sort of thing that might make people suspect you are not what you are pretending to be."

There were plenty of pairs of suede and kid gloves and silk stockings which Alina had never expected to own.

There were also nightgowns and *negligées* as well as petticoats trimmed with real lace.

When she looked at them, Alina sent up a little prayer of thankfulness to God.

She at last owned the lovely things she had always longed to have.

By the time she had finished packing it was quite late.

She went to bed and slept peacefully.

Mrs. Banks from the village came in early in the morning to prepare her breakfast.

She looked in surprise at the pile of luggage.

"You goin' away, Miss?" she enquired.

"I am going to stay with some friends," Alina said, "but I hope, Mrs. Banks, you will come in and look after the house, and I will arrange for the Vicar to pay you your money every week."

Yesterday Denise had actually been on her way downstairs when Alina had said to her in a rather embarrassed manner:

"I hate to ask you, Denise, but could you possibly let me have just a few pounds so that the woman who looks after the house can be paid? Otherwise, it will get in a dreadful state."

Denise stopped on the bottom step and gave a cry of horror.

"How stupid of me to forget to give it to you!" she apologised. "Of course I have brought you some money, and remember there is plenty more whenever you need it."

"I am ashamed to ask you, when you have given me so much," Alina murmured.

"I have given you nothing that has cost me anything!" Denise said honestly. "Here is the envelope I brought ready for you."

She pulled an envelope out of her hand-bag and put it into Alina's hand.

Then she hurried to where the carriage was waiting outside and drove off.

When she opened the envelope Alina saw there were twenty-five pounds in it.

For a moment she thought it impossible to accept so much money from her Cousin.

When she saw her the next day she would give some of it back.

Then she remembered how much she owed in the village.

As soon as she was dressed she went first to the Vicarage and handed the Vicar ten pounds.

"I do not know how long I will be away," she said, "but will you please pay Mrs. Banks every week, and if there is any dilapidation to the roof, which keeps happening, will you ask Barker to come and repair it?"

"Of course I will," the Vicar said. "I am so delighted that you are having a holiday. I have been very worried about you."

"I will be with my Cousin Denise Sedgwick, with whom, you may remember, I did lessons for so many years."

"It is the best thing that could happen," the Vicar said, "and do not worry about your house or anything here. I will see to it."

He hesitated before he added:

"You have been very brave and I know things have been difficult for you. But I prayed that God would help you, and I think He has answered my prayers."

"I know He has," Alina replied. "But please, go on praying for me."

"Of course I will," the Vicar said as he smiled.

Alina then paid the Grocer, the Baker, and the Butcher.

She had, in fact, forgotten how much she owed.

There was also a bill owing to the man who had replaced some broken panes of glass in the windows.

When she went back to the house she found she had only three pounds left.

"I must try and make it last," she told herself. "I cannot keep bothering Denise for money when she has already been so kind and generous."

The carriage arrived the following morning soon after eight o'clock.

When she finally put the newly-decorated hat on top of her head she looked at herself in surprise.

It was certainly very becoming.

She had done her hair in a fashionable manner that she had seen illustrated in the *Ladies' Journal.*

The Vicar's wife often lent it to her.

Now she thought she looked exactly as Denise would expect her to.

There was no doubt that anyone seeing her for the first time would assume that she was very much older than she was.

As Denise jumped out of the carriage and came into the house, Alina waited for the verdict.

Denise took one look at her Cousin and gave a shout of delight.

"That is marvellous!" she said. "You look absolutely stunning and exactly how a chaperon should look!"

Alina had not used the cosmetics because she was afraid of over-doing them.

But as soon as they were on the road which led to the Station, Denise insisted on her powdering her nose.

She also made her add a little rouge to her lips.

"Now, that is how I want you to look from this moment onwards," she said.

Alina stared at herself in the small mirror which fitted into her hand-bag and asked nervously:

"You . . . you do not think you have used . . . too much lip-salve?"

"Too little!" Denise said firmly. "And before

we get to London I will add a touch of rouge to your cheeks."

She did this as soon as they were alone in their reserved carriage.

When Denise had finished adding the rouge to her cheeks, she said:

"What about Mama's jewellery?"

"I have on the ear-rings," Alina said quickly, "but I thought that would be enough."

"Not nearly enough," Denise said scornfully.

She had brought the jewellery in a special crocodile case which she had told Alina to carry as well as her hand-bag.

Now she looked for the case and took out two rows of pearls which she put round Alina's neck.

There was a diamond ring for her third finger and a wedding ring.

As if this was not enough, Denise added an emerald and pearl bracelet and a brooch in the shape of a butterfly.

"Will it be safe to wear them when we are travelling?" Alina asked.

"We have plenty of people looking after us," Denise replied, "including, of course, the intimidating Marquis of Teverton!"

In the excitement of preparing for the journey, Alina had forgotten about him.

Now she asked:

"Will he be with us?"

"I am afraid so," Denise answered, "but he will make quite certain he travels in another carriage on the train to Dover, and keeps to his

41

own cabin on the ship."

Alina looked surprised.

"Do not forget," Denise explained, "he does not want us, and although we have to stay in the house where he is staying, I am quite sure we will see him only passing us on the stairs."

Alina looked at her Cousin questioningly, and she said:

"I told you that Papa tricked him into taking me to Rome, and he fell without realising it into the trap Papa set for him."

"What trap?" Alina asked.

"Papa said quite casually:

" 'I suppose you are staying at the British Embassy?'

" 'Oh, no,' Cousin Marcus replied. 'I have been lent a considerable house by one of my friends. If there is one thing that bores me, it is Diplomatic Dinners!'

" 'A house?' Papa exclaimed. 'How very fortunate! As I have a great dislike of my daughter staying in Hotels, I know you will be kind enough to have Denise and her chaperon with you.' "

Denise laughed.

"You should have seen the expression on Cousin Marcus's face, but there was nothing he could say except to agree we could stay in his house."

Alina longed to say that she was going to feel very uncomfortable staying in a house where they were not welcome.

Then she knew that Denise would not listen to her.

She hoped, therefore, that the Marquis would not be as fierce as his Cousin made out.

The rest of the way to London Denise talked only of Henry Wescott.

There was a Courier waiting for them at the London terminus to see to their luggage.

He was to travel with Denise's lady's-maid in another reserved carriage.

Alina thought they were certainly doing things in style.

They did not mention Lord Teverton again until they were driving from the station to Belgrave Square in a smart carriage.

The Courier, Denise's lady's-maid, and the luggage followed in another.

"Now, do not forget," Denise said, "when you meet Cousin Marcus, be very cool, and do not let him think you are the slightest bit impressed by him. You are an important person yourself, and are not prepared to think that anyone — whoever he may be — is superior to you!"

Alina laughed.

"Oh, Denise, you do make things difficult! Can you really imagine me feeling grander than Lord Teverton, or any of the smart Society people in London?"

"You are better than he is because you are much nicer!" Denise said firmly. "But if he tries to ignore you and me, just make him aware that you in turn intend to ignore him!"

Alina thought this was quite impossible, but there was no point in saying so.

They arrived at the impressive house in Belgrave Square.

Alina noticed as she entered it that there was a Butler with four footmen in attendance in the Hall.

The Butler bowed to them and led them across the Hall into what was obviously a Study.

It was a very elegant room, the walls lined with books.

Sitting at a flat-topped Regency desk by the window was the intimidating Lord Teverton.

At first glance Alina thought he was far better-looking than she had expected.

When he rose, and it seemed almost reluctantly, she could understand what Denise felt about him.

"Here we are, Cousin Marcus!" Denise said brightly, as if there were no awkwardness in the situation. "And let me introduce you to Lady Langley, who is being kind enough to take me with her to Rome."

Lord Teverton held out his hand to Denise, then turned towards Alina.

She thought she saw a faint flicker of surprise in his eyes before he said:

"How d'you do, Lady Langley! I do not think we have met before."

"It is unlikely," Alina said in what she hoped was a somewhat crushing tone, "as I live in the Country."

They shook hands and Lord Teverton said, drawling the words:

"I think we should leave at once for the station, and I have arranged that we will eat luncheon in the train. My Chef has prepared it for us."

"That is good news!" Denise remarked. "Papa has always said you have the best Chef in London."

"I make certain that is true," Lord Teverton said in the same lofty manner. "Now, let us be on our way."

He opened the door for them to leave the Study first.

Alina saw with amusement that one footman was holding his hat, another his travelling-cloak, a third his gloves, and a fourth his stick.

The Butler ushered them down the steps and into the carriage.

It was then Alina realised that Lord Teverton was not driving with them, but was alone in a carriage behind theirs.

Another vehicle containing his luggage and Valet was drawn up beside the one that contained Denise's lady's-maid.

Because she could not imagine anyone travelling in such state, she wanted to laugh.

She managed, however, to suppress her feeling until the carriage doors were closed and the horses moved off.

Then she said to Denise:

"This is just like a Funeral procession!"

They both laughed until the tears came into their eyes.

"I knew you would think it funny," Denise said. "You can see how furious Cousin Marcus is at having to escort us to Rome."

"I think the whole thing is ridiculous!" Alina giggled. "Can you imagine the necessity for four carriages for only six people?"

They laughed again until Denise said:

"We must be serious! I am sure Cousin Marcus will assume it is the way we behave when we are at home."

"I only hope he never sees me there," Alina said.

"I am quite certain he would not be interested enough to do that," Denise remarked. "I have learned that he is having a tremendous affair with the lovely Countess Gray, who is definitely one of the most famous Beauties in London."

"I think I have seen a picture of her in the *Ladies' Journal*," Alina said.

"I expect you have," Denise agreed. "She is dark and very exotic-looking and has dozens of men in love with her!"

"If Lord Teverton is one of them," Alina said, "why is he leaving her to go to Rome?"

"Oh, Papa can tell you the answer to that. He often goes on special missions for Earl Granville, who is the Secretary of State for Foreign Affairs."

Alina looked surprised.

"That sounds adventurous and exciting!"

"I doubt it," Denise said. "I expect he only has

to talk privately to a King, or the Pope, or somebody like that. Then, when he brings back a favourable answer, he will get another decoration on his evening-coat. It is almost covered with them already!"

Because it sounded so funny, they both started laughing again.

They arrived at the station.

As His Lordship had driven there alone, Alina was not surprised to find they had separate carriages on the train to Dover.

They were escorted by the Station-Master, resplendent in his uniform with a cap ornamented with gold braid.

They were bowed into their reserved carriage.

The door of Alina and Denise's carriage was locked so that it was impossible for anyone to intrude on them.

The Courier saw that a large hamper was placed on one of the empty seats before he withdrew to his carriage.

Lord Teverton did not come to enquire if they were comfortable, or to ask if there was anything he could do for them.

He entered the carriage which had been reserved solely for him.

Alina thought it was really rather rude of him.

She could see that her Cousin was right in saying that His Lordship resented being accompanied by two women he did not want.

"Now we can enjoy ourselves," Denise said,

"and you can take off your hat. This is an Express train, so no-one will see you until we reach Dover."

Alina did as she suggested.

Then, as Denise opened the hamper, she realised they were really living in luxury.

Alina was very hungry.

She had eaten a very small breakfast and had had only an egg which she had cooked for herself for supper.

The hamper contained everything a *gourmet* could enjoy.

There was a delicious *pâté*, lobster claws, cold chicken, and salad with a Hollandaise sauce. This was followed by a pudding of chocolate and cream that was so rich it would be impossible to manage a second helping, however one felt.

There was champagne to drink and coffee in a hay-box which kept it warm.

"If we are to eat like this every day," Alina said as they finished, "I shall never be able to get into any of my clothes because, as you know, Mama was very slim."

"And you are too thin," Denise answered. "I am sure you have been economising on food."

"Not economising," Alina replied, "just unable to afford anything that was expensive."

Denise put her hand on Alina's.

"That is all over now, dearest," she said. "I am going to look after you in the future, and you will never be hungry — or lonely — again."

In the next carriage Lord Teverton ate very little luncheon but drank several glasses of champagne.

He had been with the Countess Gray until it was nearly dawn.

He had, therefore, when he was called, awoken in a bad temper.

To begin with, he had no wish to go to Rome.

He had, however, been unable to refuse the Secretary of State for Foreign Affairs when he had begged him to do so.

"You know, Teverton, you have been so much more successful with the King and his Advisers than any of our Diplomats."

"What about the Ambassador?" Lord Teverton asked.

"You know without my saying so what I think about him," Lord Granville said. "So for goodness sake stop prevaricating and assist me. I would not have asked you if it was not urgent."

Lord Teverton sighed.

"Very well," he said. "But this is the last time you ask me to leave London just when I am enjoying myself."

"She is very attractive," Lord Granville said, "and you will not be away long."

"I will take good care of that!" Lord Teverton remarked.

He had therefore been all the more furious when he had been obliged out of sheer politeness to accept the request of Denise's father, not only

49

to escort her to Rome, but also to have her to stay in his house there.

"What does she want to go to Rome for?" he had asked. "After all, from what I hear, your daughter has been a great success in London."

"An enormous success!" the Honourable Rupert Sedgwick replied. "But she has set her heart on going to Rome, and I find it difficult to refuse."

To refuse was what Lord Teverton also wanted to do, but he had the same difficulty.

'Here I am,' he thought, 'saddled with a boring *débutante* who will chatter away without having a sensible idea in her head, and a chaperon, who will doubtless be a middle-aged old body who will make every possible excuse to gush over me.'

That happened far too often with women who toadied to him because he was so good-looking, and because he was so rich.

He enjoyed his importance.

He was well aware that Earl Granville was not the only Minister who sought his advice and his help when the occasion arose.

He often thought that if he had been a poor man, he would have gone into the Secret Service because that work intrigued and amused him.

As it was, he found himself more and more in demand by Ministers.

They realised that he knew how to manage foreigners far better than most of those in the

Foreign Office, who were paid to do so.

As the train gathered speed and Lord Teverton sipped his third glass of champagne, he thought Lady Langley was something of a surprise.

He had certainly not expected anyone so unusually lovely.

In fact, she was beautiful in a different way from any woman he had met previously.

He could not quite explain to himself the difference, but knew it was there.

Then he told himself that in some extraordinary way she looked something more than human.

He was used to women with flashing eyes, pouting lips, and an inviting expression which told him without words what they wanted.

He had the strange feeling that Lady Langley would never look like that.

Then he told himself he was not in the least interested in his unwelcome guests, and the less he saw of them, the better.

In fact, now that he thought about it, there was no reason why he should see them at all.

He had things to do in Rome which certainly did not concern them.

He was quite certain that their friends in Rome would have no points of contact with his.

Because he was going to Rome, he was reminded of the beauty of the Princess Cecilia Borghese.

When he had last seen her he had been well

aware that she found him attractive, just as he found her very beautiful.

She was the wife of the reigning Prince Borghese.

Unless his memory was at fault, the Prince was constantly called away from Rome with interests which did not at all concern his wife.

There was a faint smile on Lord Teverton's hard lips.

He thought that as a relief from the task set for him by the Earl Granville he would call at the Borghese Palace.

He was quite certain he would be welcome.

The train steamed on and Lord Teverton found his head nodding.

He had not had more than three hours sleep last night.

As often happened when he left a warm bed for the cold dawn, he wondered if the pleasures he had enjoyed with the lovely Lady Gray had been worthwhile.

It was this question of his impulses and desires which invariably brought his *affaires de coeur* to an end far sooner than expected.

If he was honest, he found that however lovely were the women he pursued and who pursued him, they were all exactly alike.

"What do I want?" Lord Teverton asked himself. "What am I looking for?"

It was a question which far too often came at dawn.

When day broke he would feel, although it

was ridiculous, that he was disillusioned and somewhat cynical.

Because he was intelligent, he tried to laugh at himself.

'A cynic at thirty!' he thought. 'In which case, what shall I be like at forty?'

He did not want to know the answer.

All he wanted was to feel that his life was full, complete, and there was nothing wanting, nothing he could not attain.

Inevitably he found his brain, as always disastrously critical, would ask the same questions, especially after a night of passion.

"What am I looking for? Where am I going? What is my ultimate goal?"

It was a case of having had too much too soon, his mind told him.

He wished that he could turn off the self-examination as another man might turn off a tap.

But it continued.

Then he knew as the train seemed to go even faster that although it seemed extraordinary even to him, he would not be seeking out Lady Gray when he returned.

chapter three

When they reached Calais, Lord Teverton was annoyed.

He realised he would have to share his special Drawing-Room carriage, which was attached to the Rome train, with his Cousin and her chaperon.

He had crossed the Channel in peace and quiet, sitting in his own cabin reading *The Times* and *The Morning Post*.

He had not really thought about the journey to Rome until they disembarked.

He carried out many diplomatic missions and he was also a very rich man.

He therefore always travelled in the same style and comfort as Queen Victoria.

He had a Drawing-Room carriage specially attached to the train.

It consisted of a comfortable Sitting-Room with a sofa and arm-chairs, and two bedrooms.

If he was travelling alone with his Valet, his Valet had a bed put up in the space provided to accommodate the luggage.

On this journey his Valet and Denise's lady's-maid would have an ordinary carriage reserved for themselves.

What annoyed him when he boarded the train

was to remember that of the two bed-rooms, one was larger than the other.

The former, of course, was the one he always occupied.

Now a second bed had been installed in it so that it could be shared by his Cousin and her chaperon.

He went into the smaller sleeping-compartment and thought that women were a nuisance, especially when they were connected with him only by birth.

There was, however, nothing he could do about it.

He changed from his travelling-clothes into something more comfortable.

Alina, like Denise, was delighted with the Drawing-Room carriage.

"I have never been in one before," Denise said, "but Papa has told me how the Queen travels, and he himself had a carriage like this when he went to Vienna with Mama."

"It is delightful!" Alina exclaimed. "I love the comfortable chairs and the sofa. And although we are going to be rather cramped in the sleeping-compartment, it will be fun to be with you."

"Of course it will," Denise agreed, "but we must be careful what we say in front of Cousin Marcus."

They took off their hats and cloaks and Alina said:

"Let us change. We have been in the same clothes all day, and this gown is rather tight."

"You look very pretty in it," Denise answered, "but let us change. Can you remember in which trunk the gown you want is packed?"

It was a difficult question.

It took Alina some time to find a simple, thin afternoon-gown which she thought suitable for dinner on a train.

Denise put on one of the white gowns she had bought in London.

When they had arranged their hair they went into the Drawing-Room.

Lord Teverton was seated in an arm-chair, reading some papers.

He looked up as they appeared and made a perfunctory gesture to rise.

"We do not wish to disturb you, Cousin Marcus," Denise said quickly. "If you are busy working, we can wait in our sleeping-compartment until dinner is ready."

"It is being prepared now," Lord Teverton replied, "so sit down, as the train will soon be increasing speed."

He spoke with his usual drawl, as if it were an effort to talk to Denise.

When he was not looking, she made a grimace at Alina.

They had hardly seated themselves before Stevens, Lord Teverton's Valet, and a steward brought in dinner.

They would move into their own compartment when the train stopped at a station.

As Alina had expected, Lord Teverton had brought the dinner with him from London.

It was just as delicious as the luncheon they had on the way to Dover.

Lord Teverton also had a small glass of brandy when the meal was finished.

They talked very little at first. Then Alina said to Denise:

"I am looking forward to seeing Rome. I have read about its history, but I never thought I would see the treasures about which I have read with my own eyes!"

"You have read about Rome?" Lord Teverton asked before Denise could speak.

"Many, many books about it," Alina replied.

She was thinking that it had been one of her Father's favourite places.

He had talked to her about the Forum and all the buildings which had been the background to the formation of the great Roman Empire.

"I am surprised," Lord Teverton replied.

Alina looked at him.

"That I should be interested particularly in Rome, or that I should read any serious books?" she enquired defensively.

There was a faintly mocking smile on his lips as he replied:

"Both."

"That is so unfair!" Alina objected. "If I were a man, you would have expected me to be interested in Roman History and the astonishing way in which their Empire expanded, to include even England."

She made a gesture with her hand before she went on:

"But because I am a woman you assume immediately that I read only the *Ladies' Journal* and occasionally a novel."

Lord Teverton laughed, and it was a genuine sound of humour.

"I apologise! Of course I apologise," he said. "But most of the women I have known do, as you say, read magazines from cover to cover and find little time to read anything else."

"Then I hope you will be more generous to my sex in the future," Alina said, "for I assure you I am not the only woman who is interested in History. But perhaps they do not move in the social circles you patronise."

"Touché!" Lord Teverton remarked, and his eyes were twinkling.

Denise was listening, entranced.

Alina was behaving just as she wanted her to do.

She thought it was very good for her stuck-up Cousin to be challenged by a woman instead of their fawning all over him as they usually did.

Lord Teverton demanded to test Alina to see if she really had read the History of Rome.

He spoke first of St. Peter's Basilica of which, as it happened, she knew a great deal.

"I always think," she said, "it is a wonderful story how Constantine the Great, the first

Christian Emperor, built the first Basilica of St. Peter over the actual spot where St. Peter was buried after he had been martyred in the reign of Nero."

Denise, watching, realised that her Cousin Marcus raised his eye-brows as if he were surprised, and was temporarily silenced.

Alina went on, following her own thoughts:

"The one thing I really want to see in Rome more than anything else is the Fountain of Trevi."

"Now you are being more feminine," Lord Teverton remarked. "I have never met a woman yet who did not want to make a wish in the fountain."

"How do you have to wish in it?" Denise asked.

"It was built by Nicolò Salvi in 1762," Lord Teverton replied. "It is very beautiful and reputed to be extremely lucky. Anyone who throws two coins into the fountain standing with their back to it has two wishes."

"How exciting!" Denise exclaimed.

"One is that you will return to Rome," Alina took up the story, "the second is your personal wish which, unless the Story-Tellers lie, is always fulfilled."

Denise clasped her hands together.

"Then that is the first place we will go!"

"Of course," Alina answered.

She knew exactly what her Cousin would wish for.

As she looked at Denise, she guessed she was thinking rapturously of Henry Wescott.

"I think perhaps you are raising Denise's hopes unduly," Lord Teverton drawled. "After all, I cannot believe that everybody who wishes at the Trevi Fountain is so fortunate."

Alina threw up her hands.

"You are not to spoil our illusions," she said. "You have been to Rome before, but for Denise and myself it is an adventure, and we want to believe in everything, enjoy everything, and be very, very grateful for having the opportunity to be there."

She spoke so sincerely that Lord Teverton was again silent.

He could not help thinking that Lady Langley was very different from what he had expected.

She was totally different from the many women he had known in London.

He thought the enthusiasm in her voice was touching.

He was sure that because she had lived in the Country she was unspoilt.

Everything she saw would be exciting for her.

At the same time, he was genuinely overwhelmed by her beauty.

He had thought her lovely the first time he had seen her.

Now, without a hat, she looked younger and even more beautiful.

He wondered how old she was, but knew it was a question he could not ask.

She had certainly, he thought, had a very generous husband.

Denise saw his eyes on the necklace she had put round Alina's long neck after she had changed her gown.

It was a small one, otherwise it would have been out of place on a train-journey.

But the diamonds were a blue-white and matched the ear-rings and the brooch Alina wore on her breast.

Denise smiled to herself, thinking her Cousin Marcus was being completely deceived, exactly as she wanted him to be.

She told herself she had been very clever.

Once launched on an historical discussion, Alina found it difficult not to continue.

She had missed her Father so desperately after he was killed because he had always talked to her as if she were his contemporary.

They had entered into intellectual discussions on many different subjects.

History had been their favourite, but her Mother had taken no part in the cut and thrust of their debates.

Lady Langley had been quite content to listen to the two people she loved.

She would tell them when it was all over how clever they both were.

"We shall have to be careful, darling," she had said once to her husband, "Otherwise Alina will become a 'blue-stocking,' and you know how frightened men are of a woman who is too clever."

"If a woman is that clever," her husband replied, "she will not let a man feel inferior to her, however stupid he may be!"

Alina and her Mother had laughed at this.

But after her Father's death Alina had thought despairingly that never again would she enjoy similar intellectual discussions.

Now she found herself enjoying an argument with Lord Teverton.

It was not only that she was obeying Denise's instructions to stand up to him and make him be impressed with her.

However, it had been a very long day, and when Denise yawned, Alina knew it was time they went to bed.

"What time do we arrive in Rome?" she asked Lord Teverton.

"Late in the afternoon," he replied, "so there will be no need for you to hurry up for breakfast, although Stevens will have it ready at about nine o'clock."

"Anyhow, do not wait for us," Denise said.

"I have no intention of doing so," Lord Teverton replied.

Now he was drawling again in the way she most disliked.

When they went into their sleeping-compartment, Denise said in a whisper:

"You were splendid! But you do see how he treats me? As if I were still in the cradle!"

"I agree with you, he is rather frightening," Alina said.

"But you stood up to him," Denise said as she smiled, "and he was obviously surprised that you were so intelligent."

They undressed and got into bed.

When Lord Teverton went to his own compartment he could hear his two companions laughing together.

He thought it was a very young sound.

He was used to women who had been told their laughter was like the tinkling of bells, though it was in fact always contrived.

The two women in the adjoining sleeping-compartment sounded like School-girls.

"It is obvious in some ways that Lady Langley comes from the Country," he said. "At the same time, although she is not aware of it, she would be a sensation in London!"

He had noticed the graceful way she walked.

He knew that with her strange beauty, the Prince of Wales would find her entrancing.

Then he thought it would be a shame for her to be spoilt.

She was like a Lily-of-the-Valley.

It would be a mistake to change her into an orchid, which was exotic in its own way but had no fragrance.

'Dammit all, I am becoming poetical!' he thought. 'The sooner I get to Rome and contact the Princess, the better!'

When he was in bed he found himself lying awake.

He was listening to the voices he could still hear even above the rattle of the train.

He did not know what they were saying.

Yet the lilt and youth of their voices was recognisable.

It was a long time before he fell asleep.

The next day Alina was thrilled by what she could see from the window.

She made no effort to talk to Lord Teverton after they had had breakfast, which surprised him.

He was used to women, even before he showed any interest in them, looking at him expectantly.

They then did everything in their power to attract his attention.

Alina, on the contrary, had just gone to a comfortable chair by the window.

She was absorbed in looking out at the countryside through which they were passing.

She occasionally exclaimed to Denise:

"Oh, look at those peasants working in the fields!" or "Do look at that exquisite Villa! I am sure it is still occupied by a Nobleman whose family have inherited it for centuries."

Lord Teverton, reading the papers which required his attention before he reached Rome, could not help listening.

They had already crossed the border into Italy and the countryside was quite different.

Alina was thrilled by the tall spires of the

Churches, the structure of the houses, and the picturesque villages.

"I can see," Lord Teverton remarked somewhat mockingly as they sat down to luncheon, "that you intend to be an ardent sight-seer when we reach Rome."

"But of course!" Alina replied. "It would be very foolish if I did not visit everything I can and store it in my memory in case I never have the chance to return."

"So your Trevi wish may not come true!" Lord Teverton said as if he had scored a point.

"Then I shall return in another life," Alina said, "and doubtless I was a Roman in a life before this one."

Lord Teverton found it impossible not to challenge her belief in reincarnation.

They were arguing fiercely.

Unexpectedly, like everything else she did, Alina insisted on sitting by the window.

"In case," she explained, "I miss anything important in the scenery."

Lord Teverton picked up his papers again.

As he did so, he told himself he could never remember an occasion when a woman to whom he was giving his full attention found the scenery, or anything else, more interesting than him.

'Lady Langley is certainly unusual,' he thought cynically.

By the time they arrived in Rome they were tired.

As the train was late, it was dark before they

reached the house which Lord Teverton had been lent.

It was larger than Alina had expected and situated near the top of the Spanish Steps.

She learnt soon after she arrived that the magnificent Park on one side of it was known also as Villa Borghese.

She had read about the beautiful Princess Pauline Borghese, who had been Napoleon Bonaparte's sister.

The memory of what she had read about her came back.

Now she found herself excited by the idea that they were not very far from the Palazzo Borghese, which lay below them near the River Tiber.

Then she sighed as she thought:

'I am not likely to enter it, although perhaps I shall see it as we pass.'

Denise was thinking only of Henry Wescott and asking Alina a thousand times how she should get in touch with him.

"Whatever happens," she kept saying, "he must not think I have come here especially to see him."

"You know where he is staying?" Alina asked.

"Yes, of course. He is with his Grandmother, the Dowager Countess, who lives in Rome because the climate suits her so much better than that of England."

She smiled before she added:

"I also think she dislikes the idea of seeing her grandson in her husband's place, although she keeps telling Henry he should marry and have a family."

"And that is, of course, exactly what he should do!" Alina agreed.

Finally they decided that Denise should send the Earl a short note.

She could tell him she had arrived in Rome to keep her friend Lady Langley company, and it would be fun to see him again.

It took some time to compose the note.

Before they went to bed they handed it to a servant and asked him to take it to the Dowager Countess's villa first thing in the morning.

When Denise kissed Alina good-night she said:

"You are praying? Tell me you are praying, Alina, that everything will be all right."

"Of course I am, dearest," Alina replied, "and you are not to worry. We will go to the Trevi Fountain first thing in the morning, throw our coins in the water, and wish that you and Henry will live happily ever after."

"I do believe that whatever you wish at the Fountain will come true — despite what Cousin Marcus said!" Denise declared.

"He is just being cynical and deliberately argumentative," Alina replied.

"I told you he was awful," Denise reminded her.

"Not awful," Alina corrected her Cousin. "I can see he is clever, but for some reason that I cannot understand I think he despises women."

"Despises them?" Denise queried. "Good Heavens! He is always making love to some woman or other! I have listened to the Mothers of the other girls talking about him, and my Grandmother, who presented me, warned me that he was the 'Casanova of London,' and she hoped I never married a man like that."

"I can understand it would be misery," Alina agreed, "but I did rather enjoy arguing with him."

"It is an enjoyment you will not experience again," Denise said. "He made it clear, when Papa arranged for us to stay in his house, that he would not be able to give us a minute of his time."

Alina laughed.

"I am sure we will manage quite well in Rome without him. So go to sleep and believe, even before we start wishing, that everything will come true."

It might have been a prophecy!

Next morning, just after they had finished breakfast, the Earl arrived.

He was, Alina thought with relief when he entered the room, extremely prepossessing.

Very English-looking, he had a frank, open face that she liked.

He was announced after they had left the Dining-Room and had moved into the Sitting-Room.

They were deciding what they should do during the day.

Lord Teverton, needless to say, had breakfast alone, and they had not seen him when they came downstairs.

Now, as the Earl walked across the room, Alina was sure the expression in his eyes was one of love.

"How is it possible that you are here?" he asked Denise. "I never imagined you would come to Rome."

With difficulty Denise had suppressed a cry of delight when he was announced.

Now she managed to say in quite a casual manner:

"Oh, Lady Langley asked me to come with her, and it seemed too good an opportunity to miss."

She turned to Alina, saying:

"I do not think you have met the Earl of Wescott."

"How do you do?" the Earl said politely. "May I welcome you to Rome — and it is delightful to have Denise here."

"Thank you," Alina said, "and we are just planning all the things we want to see."

As she spoke, she turned towards Denise and said:

"Forgive me, dearest, if I just go upstairs and fetch that book I was telling you about. It has very good descriptions of the places we want to visit, and it will help us to decide our programme."

"Shall I fetch it for you?" Denise asked.

"I think I had better go myself," Alina replied. "I am not quite certain in which trunk I put it, and I shall have to instruct the maid."

She went from the room as she spoke, feeling she had been very tactful.

As soon as Henry Wescott closed the door behind her he walked back toward Denise.

She was standing beside the fireplace.

She did not speak, but waited until he was standing beside her.

"Have you come here to torture me?" he asked.

"I . . . I do not know . . . what you mean," Denise replied.

"You drove me mad!" he declared. "I came away because I intended never to see you again."

"How could . . . you be so . . . unkind?"

"Did it seem unkind to you — or were you glad I had gone?"

"Of course I was not . . . glad! I could not . . . believe you would do anything so . . . cruel as to just . . . leave me for no reason . . . whatsoever."

"There was reason enough as far as I was concerned," Henry said. "You were behaving abominably with Charles Patterson, and, short of killing him in a duel, there was nothing I could do about it."

He spoke aggressively.

Then suddenly Denise could no longer keep up the pretence.

"Can we . . . forget about . . . Charles?" she

asked in a low voice. "I was so . . . happy before . . . you became so . . . angry."

"Is that true?" Henry asked.

"I swear to you it is."

Their eyes met and they were both very still.

"I love you!" Henry said. "You know that. But I want you to love me too."

Denise wanted to answer, but somehow the words would not come to her lips.

It was then, as if he had to know the truth, Henry put his arms round her.

He drew her close to him.

Her lips were waiting for his, and as he kissed her he knew there was no need for words, no need for explanations.

He kissed her until the world seemed to spin dizzily round them.

When he raised his head, Denise put her face against his neck.

"Oh . . . Henry!" she said in a broken little voice.

"You love me!" he said triumphantly. "You love me! Now tell me you will marry me."

Because she had wanted him so desperately and been terribly afraid it would not happen, Denise felt the tears come into her eyes.

Very gently Henry put his fingers under her chin and turned her face up to his.

When he saw her tears and that her lips were trembling, he looked at her for a long moment.

Then he pulled her a little closer.

"We will be very happy," he said.

Then his lips were on hers.

Upstairs Alina finished unpacking her trunks.

She arranged her new clothes so that she would be able to know herself exactly where they were.

Then she looked out of the window.

She wondered how long Denise would be downstairs.

She was longing to go out and discover Rome.

There was so much to see, so much to do, and she thought she could not bear to miss a minute of it.

Time seemed to pass very slowly.

She was beginning to wonder if she would have to stay the rest of the morning in her bedroom.

Then the door burst open and Denise rushed in.

She flung her arms around Alina, saying:

"It is all right! Everything is all right! He loves me . . . he loves me and we are to be married! Oh, Alina . . . I am so happy."

Alina kissed her.

"And I am so happy for you."

"We are going now to visit Henry's Grandmother, and he wants you to come too," Denise said.

"I am sure you do not want me," Alina replied.

"Henry says his Grandmother is a stickler for convention, and would think it scandalous if he and I should arrive in a carriage together without a chaperon!"

"Then of course I will come with you," Alina

said. "I hope I look respectable enough for the Dowager Countess."

"Put on your most impressive hat," Denise said, "while I go and dress."

She ran to her own bed-room.

Alina did as she was told and took the most elaborate of the hats she had re-trimmed out of the wardrobe.

Picking up her hand-bag and gloves, she hoped that the Dowager Countess would be impressed.

Denise was in a hurry to be with Henry, so she managed to change into one of her best gowns in only a few minutes.

When they went downstairs together, Henry was waiting for them in the Hall.

Alina held out her hand.

"I must congratulate you, My Lord," she said, "and I know that you and Denise will be very happy."

"Thank you," the Earl said, smiling, "we shall, I promise you, be blissfully happy once we are married. But my Grandmother will want to give a party for us, or perhaps several, before we leave Rome."

Alina felt her heart leap.

She had been desperately afraid while she was waiting for Denise.

She was thinking that if she and Henry were engaged, they would have to return immediately to England.

Now she hoped there would be at least a few days in which to see everything she wanted to see.

The Earl had arrived in an open carriage drawn by two horses which was waiting for them.

The coachman and the footman were on the box.

They set off, but Henry and Denise could only sit looking at each other.

Alina thought it would be difficult to find two people who were more in love.

She was so glad that her prayers had been answered.

At the same time, she knew that every second that was passing was precious because she was in Rome.

However many wishes she might make at the Trevi Fountain, she was certain that it would never be possible for her to come here again.

"This is the Park known as the Villa Borghese," the Earl was saying as they drove along the road, "and actually we are dining at the Palace to-night."

"Dining there?" Denise asked.

"The Prince and Princess invited my Grandmother some time ago, and she was delighted by the idea, especially as I am staying with her. Now, of course, she will ask if we may bring you and Lady Langley to the party as well as Lord Teverton."

Alina felt excited.

She had read about the Borghese Palace, how it contained the most marvellous collection of treasures in the whole of Rome.

It had been started in 1605 by Cardinal Camillo Borghese before he became Pope.

She had never thought she would have the chance of seeing inside the Palace.

Now she knew it was the most exciting thing that had ever happened to her.

She wanted to tell the Earl so.

Then, when she turned her face towards him, she saw that he was looking at Denise.

They were in an enchanted world of their own.

chapter four

The Dowager Countess lived in a very luxurious Villa surrounded by a large garden.

She was nearly eighty, but still had remains of the beauty which had made her famous.

She obviously adored her grandson.

After they had had luncheon, waited on by efficient if ancient servants, the Earl took Denise into the garden.

When they were alone, the Dowager Countess said to Alina:

"I am delighted that Henry is marrying such a charming young girl. I have been eager for him to settle down and get married."

"He could not have chosen a lovelier bride," Alina said, "and Denise is truly in love with him."

The Dowager Countess clasped her hands together.

"That is what I wanted to hear. I have always been so afraid that he would be married for his title and his money."

"I know they are ecstatically in love with each other," Alina said, "and that is all that matters."

"Of course," the Dowager Countess agreed.

She then looked at Alina and said:

"I do not remember meeting you, or any of your family, when I lived in England."

"We have always lived very quietly in the Country," Alina said quickly.

"That would account for it," the Dowager Countess said, "and that is what I hope Henry and Denise will do."

She was obviously interested in nothing but her grandson.

Alina gave a little sigh of relief.

She had been afraid that she might be cross-questioned by English people.

They could easily think she looked too young for the part she was playing.

They stayed with the Dowager Countess until she was beginning to look tired.

Alina was certain that, living in Italy, she had adopted the custom of the Country of taking a short *siesta* after luncheon.

She therefore signalled to Denise that they should leave.

The Dowager Countess did not press them to stay.

When they were outside the door Denise asked:

"Would you mind if Henry and I go to St. Peter's? We want to pray that our marriage will be a happy one."

"That is exactly what you should do," Alina agreed, "and of course I do not mind. I will walk back to the house."

"You will do nothing of the sort," Henry said firmly.

He hailed a Hackney carriage that was

standing in the Square a little way from the Villa.

As he did so, Denise said to Alina in a low voice:

"I do not think you have any Italian money."

"I had forgotten that," Alina replied.

She had only what she had brought with her from England.

When Henry was not looking, Denise slipped several Italian notes into her hand.

Then she jumped into Henry's carriage and they drove off.

Alina got into the Hackney carriage.

When the driver asked her where she wanted to go, she answered in Italian.

She told him the address of the house where they were staying.

Then she had a sudden idea.

"I have changed my mind," she said. "I want to go to the Trevi Fountain."

There was no need to give the address.

The Italian grinned and whipped up his horse.

The carriage was open.

Alina enjoyed the sunshine, the crowded streets, and the trees coming into bloom.

Everything about Rome was so lovely.

She only hoped she would have a chance to see everything before Denise and Henry were ready to return to England.

It took a little time, because the narrow streets were crowded, to reach the Trevi Fountain.

Alina realised it was impossible to drive right up to it.

The carriage stopped in a road from which there was a pavement leading to the Fountain.

Alina thought she could find her way back to the house at the top of the Spanish Steps.

She therefore paid the coachman what he asked and put the change into her hand-bag.

Feeling excited, she walked through the passage which took her to the front of the Fountain.

There were only a few people on the two rows of stone steps.

They were sitting looking at the water pouring out from beneath a huge statue of Neptune.

He was in a wheeled chariot drawn by two horses.

For a moment Alina could only stand staring at the beautiful sculpture.

The water caught the sunlight which also glittered on the coins lying in the stone basin.

She remembered that she must wish, and looked in her hand-bag.

Apart from some small Italian notes, she had three pounds of English money — two sovereigns and two half-sovereigns.

It seemed very extravagant!

Then she asked herself what could be more important than making a wish.

She remembered it was customary that the first wish should be that one would return to Rome.

However, for her, that was so unlikely it seemed a waste.

"What I shall wish for first," she decided, "is that Denise will be happy for ever with her Earl, and the other wish will be for myself."

She took out the two half-sovereigns and closed her bag.

After looking entranced at the Fountain, she turned round and closed her eyes.

Holding one half-sovereign in her right hand, she wished with all her heart, and it was a prayer that Denise would be happy.

Then she threw the coin over her shoulder.

She held the second half-sovereign in the same way.

As she shut her eyes again she knew that what she wanted was to find for herself the love that Denise and Henry had for each other, the happiness she had seen in their faces when their eyes met.

"Give me love," she wished, "real love, because I am so alone, and that is what I want to find."

She threw the coin.

As she did so, she felt her hand-bag tugged from her left hand.

For a moment she could not think what was happening.

Then as she opened her eyes she saw a small boy.

Bare-footed and wearing ragged clothes, he was leaping like a fawn over the stone steps.

Then he ran through the passage by which she had approached the Fountain.

"Stop!" she cried out in English, then again: *"Alt! Alt! Alt!"*

She ran as quickly as she could after the small boy, but he had vanished into the street outside.

She knew she could not catch him.

She stood still, feeling a sense of shock at what had occurred.

She wondered what she should do.

Suddenly a voice beside her asked in the drawl she knew so well:

"Now, what can have happened to make you look so concerned?"

It was Lord Teverton. Without even turning her head, Alina replied:

"My hand-bag has been . . . stolen with . . . all my money . . . in it!"

"That certainly is a disaster," Lord Teverton said slowly, "but I imagine you mean all the money you had brought out with you this morning."

For a moment, because she was so concerned about her loss, Alina hardly realised what he was saying.

Then after a short pause she said:

"Y-yes . . . yes of course . . . that is what I mean. How could I have been so . . . foolish as to . . . close my . . . eyes?"

"You were wishing at the Fountain?" Lord Teverton asked. "But as that is the correct ritual, you can hardly blame yourself if one of those pestilential little Gypsy boys stole your hand-bag."

"It is the . . . only one . . . I have," Alina murmured to herself.

"Then suppose we remedy the loss of something so necessary," Lord Teverton said. "I will drive you to a shop not far from here, where I believe they have the best selection of bags in the whole of Rome."

Quite suddenly Alina realised what he was saying.

She could not afford to buy a hand-bag, nor had she now any money to put in it.

"No . . . no . . . of course . . . not," she said. "I am sure Denise will . . . lend me . . . one."

"My Chaise is very close," Lord Teverton persisted. "It would be no trouble to take you to the shop, and it is in fact on our way home."

"I would much rather . . . return to the house," Alina said.

She was thinking frantically what excuse she could give for not going shopping.

Then the words came to her lips.

"I think Denise will be back by now, and I came to the . . . Fountain only on an . . . impulse."

"I learnt at the house you had gone out to luncheon with Wescott," Lord Teverton said, "so I suppose Denise is still with him. I feel sure they can manage quite well without you. Incidentally, why are you alone?"

"Denise and the Earl have gone to St. Peter's."

"St. Peter's?" Lord Teverton exclaimed in astonishment. "Why should they do that?"

"Oh, I forgot — you do not know," Alina said. "It all happened so suddenly, but this morning soon after breakfast the Earl called on Denise, and they have now become engaged to be married."

"That is a surprise!" Lord Teverton said.

He thought for a moment, then added:

"I presume that is the reason why she was so eager to come to Rome."

Alina thought this was uncomfortably perceptive of him, and she said:

"They are very happy, and I came to the Fountain to make a wish that their happiness would last for ever."

"Very commendable and unselfish of you," Lord Teverton said mockingly. "But surely you also wished for yourself?"

He was much too perceptive, Alina thought.

He was looking at her in a penetrating way, and she knew with annoyance that she was blushing.

She could see a little way ahead of them the Chaise in which he must have arrived.

"It would be very kind if you would drive me back," she said quickly, "just in case I am wanted."

"Of course!"

He helped her into the Chaise, then got into the driver's seat.

The groom who had been holding the two horses sprang up into the small seat behind.

Lord Teverton drove the Chaise skilfully but

carefully through the throng of vehicles, all of which seemed to be converging on the entrance to the Fountain.

As they moved into a wider street, he said:

"So you had luncheon with Wescott — where?"

"With his Grandmother, the Dowager Countess," Alina replied.

"I remember her," Lord Teverton remarked, "a charming woman who must have been very beautiful in her day."

"That is what I thought," Alina said.

"Shall I prophesy," he went on, "that you will be very beautiful for many years? It will be a very long time before old age withers you, as it must do eventually."

Alina glanced at him in surprise, and he said:

"You must be aware that you look very young. I suppose you would not care to tell me your age?"

"Of course not!" Alina replied quickly. "I have always been told that it is very rude to speculate about a lady's age!"

"Not when she looks as young as you, Lady Langley," Lord Teverton said. "At the same time, Denise tells me you had been happily married for many years."

Alina thought this was becoming a more and more uncomfortable conversation, and after a moment she said:

"How lovely Rome is! Every house in the street is a picture in itself! And the Fountain was far more beautiful than I expected."

"You are changing the subject," Lord Teverton said accusingly. "I thought every woman liked to talk about herself."

"Then I must be the exception," Alina said. "I have no wish to talk about myself, but about Rome."

There was a twinkle in Lord Teverton's eyes as he drove on.

He was thinking that any other woman with whom he was alone would have said they wished to talk about him.

They were once again driving through very narrow streets.

As he had to negotiate his horses carefully, both he and Alina were silent.

Only as they climbed up the hill towards the house in which they were staying did she say:

"I expect Denise will tell you that we are all dining to-night at the Borghese Palace."

Lord Teverton raised his eye-brows.

He had, in fact, been on his way to call at the Borghese Palace himself.

But he had seen Lady Langley driving in a Hackney carriage towards the Fountain and had decided, out of curiosity, to follow her.

He had had luncheon with the British Ambassador, which he had found very boring.

He had then intended to go to the Borghese Palace.

He was actually waiting until it was the correct time to call on the Princess.

Alina was explaining to him that a special party had been arranged for the Dowager Countess.

"While we were having luncheon with her," she went on, "she sent a message to the Princess to say that her grandson was engaged to Denise, although it was a secret that would not be announced until they were back in England. However, she was sure the Princess would not mind if she brought Denise, you, and myself to the party to-night."

"I am sure Her Highness will be delighted," Lord Teverton said. "She is known to be a very generous hostess."

"I am so excited at the thought of seeing the Borghese Palace," Alina said. "I thought I should never have the opportunity."

"Well, now you will see it in style," Lord Teverton answered, "and let me warn you that Italian women are very smart, or, as the French say, *chic*. So put on your best gown and all the dazzling frills and furbelows you possess."

He was mocking her, Alina knew, but she merely laughed and said:

"I will do my best to do credit to the Union Jack, but you must not blame me if I fail."

Lord Teverton brought his horses to a standstill outside the house.

"Thank you for bringing me home," Alina said.

He helped her out of the Chaise and she walked into the Hall.

She asked the man-servant at the door if Miss Sedgwick had returned, but he shook his head.

She then went upstairs to the bed-room.

She thought it would be a mistake to be alone with Lord Teverton in case he questioned her further about her bag.

"How could I have been so foolish?" she asked herself.

It would be embarrassing to have to borrow one of Denise's.

It was even worse to have to admit that all she had left of the money Denise had given her in England was two pounds.

Now that had been stolen.

She had not been in her room very long and had only taken off her hat when Denise appeared.

"I heard you were back," she said, "and oh, Alina, it is so beautiful in St. Peter's! I am sure that Henry and I had a very special blessing, and we will never lose each other again."

"I am sure you will not do that," Alina said as she smiled.

"Henry is downstairs talking to Cousin Marcus," Denise said. "He told us that you had your hand-bag stolen."

"Oh, dearest, I am so sorry," Alina said, "but I had wished that you and Henry would be happy together. I shut my eyes, and just as I was making my second wish a small boy snatched my bag and ran off with it."

"Well, I can easily lend you another one," Denise said. "Was there much money in it?"

There was a little pause before Alina said apologetically:

"All the money I . . . had left of what you had so kindly given me in England. Fortunately, however, I had paid all the bills at home that were owing before I came away."

"Well, that was sensible, so I suppose that horrid boy did not get very much."

"Two sovereigns . . . and one or two of the Italian notes you gave me," Alina admitted.

Denise laughed.

"Is that all there was? There is no need to cry over so little."

"I feel ashamed to keep taking money from you," Alina said, "when you have done so much for me already."

"Do not be so ridiculous," Denise replied. "Look what you have done for me. Without you I could not have come to Rome and found Henry! And you were very, very tactful in leaving us alone together, just as I wanted you to do."

She kissed Alina and said:

"Stop worrying. I am going downstairs to say good-bye to Henry. Then we have to plan what we are going to wear to-night. I can tell you it will be a very, very smart occasion."

"That is what Lord Teverton told me it would be," Alina replied.

"He is right," Denise said. "And it will be very exciting to see the Palace. But for Henry's sake we must not look like 'Country Bumpkins.' "

She paused for a moment before she went on:

"Oh, Alina, I am so happy! He is so sweet, and I want him to think me the prettiest person at the party."

"Which you will be!" Alina replied.

"I will go down and say good-bye to him, then we must have a conference about what you shall wear."

She ran from the room.

Alina thought she had never seen her look happier or more beautiful.

Because she wanted to look her best to-night, she went to the wardrobe and looked at the gowns hanging there.

Those given to her by Denise were very attractive.

But she had not yet had time to make them as elaborate as the gowns that would be worn by the older women present.

Finally Alina decided on a gown of her Mother's which had been her best.

She had worn it to a Ball given by the Lord Lieutenant and everybody had admired her.

When Denise returned, she agreed that that would be the most suitable gown for Alina to wear.

She herself intended to wear the gown in which she had been presented at Court.

It had been extremely expensive.

"I have ordered a hairdresser to come to do our hair," Denise said, "and we had better not be late or I am sure Cousin Marcus will be very disagreeable."

Alina thought he had in fact been very kind to her when she had lost her hand-bag.

Later, just as she was ready to have her bath, a parcel was brought to her room.

She thought at first the servant had made a mistake and it was intended for Denise.

But he insisted it was for her.

When she opened it she found it contained an extremely attractive hand-bag, even smarter than the one that had been stolen.

She stared at it in surprise until she saw there was a card inside.

It bore Lord Teverton's name and written on the back was:

"A present from Rome"

Now she stared at the bag in sheer astonishment.

How could Lord Teverton, of all people, give her anything so expensive and, of course, exactly what she needed?

Because she was so surprised, she ran from her room into Denise's.

"Look, Denise!" she cried. "Just look what your Cousin has given me! I can hardly believe it!"

Denise admired the hand-bag and said:

"His stuck-up Lordship has certainly 'come up trumps' for once!"

"I feel embarrassed," Alina said, "because when he suggested taking me to a shop to buy another bag, I refused. It was, of course, because I could not afford it, but perhaps he thought I was really asking for a present."

"I should not worry about that," Denise said. "Cousin Marcus can afford a million hand-bags if he wants to buy them. It is a blessing, as far as I am concerned, that he has not taken a dislike to you and made things difficult."

She laughed before Alina could reply and said:

"You know as well as I do he was furious at having us with him. If you think about it, he could hardly have been ruder on the journey, short of shutting us up in the Guard's Van!"

"He has certainly made amends for it now," Alina answered, "but perhaps I ought to refuse to accept such an expensive present."

"Oh, for goodness' sake, Alina, do not make difficulties! You never know how Cousin Marcus will react. Now that he is being pleasant, as he is to you, make the most of it!"

"But . . . I do feel embarrassed and . . . rather shy," Alina confessed.

Denise gave a cry of horror.

"That is the last thing you must feel! Do you not realise that the sort of lady with whom my Cousin spends his time would not think a hand-bag nearly good enough unless it bore her initials in diamonds and its fittings were made of pure gold!"

"I do not believe it!" Alina exclaimed.

"It is true," Denise replied. "He is expected by the Society Beauties to give them the most expensive gifts because he is so rich. I was told he gave the Countess Gray a necklace of rubies that is worth a King's ransom!"

Listening, Alina realised that in that case it would be ridiculous to make a fuss about a hand-bag.

"Take everything you can get," Denise was saying, "and do not be over-grateful or he will think you are toadying to him."

This was all good advice.

Yet, when Alina went downstairs before they left for the Borghese Palace, she felt nervous.

Although she knew that Denise would laugh at her, she nevertheless felt shy.

When she went into the Study where they were all to meet, Lord Teverton was alone.

He was looking particularly impressive, she thought, in his evening-clothes.

There were several decorations on his coat and one round his neck.

As she walked toward him she felt that he was appraising her.

She saw him look at the tiara she wore on her head, and the necklace of diamonds which matched her ear-rings and her bracelets.

He did not move, and by the time she reached him she felt breathless.

"I want to . . . thank you so . . . very much. It was very . . . kind of you to . . . give me that . . . beautiful hand-bag, and I will be very . . . careful not to . . . lose it."

She had no idea that her cheeks were flushed

as she spoke, and her eye-lashes flickered.

"No more wishes!" Lord Teverton admonished. "And if you must shut your eyes, beware of small boys!"

"I shall be very . . . very . . . careful in the . . . future," Alina promised.

"May I tell you," he said, "that you are looking very beautiful? I will be extremely proud of the two ladies I am escorting to the Borghese Palace."

"You have said exactly the right thing," Alina replied, "because Denise wants to shine so as to impress the Earl."

Lord Teverton smiled.

"I think Henry Wescott is quite impressed enough already. He is obviously very much in love!"

"That is exactly what he should be," Alina said.

"It is what would be expected in Rome," Lord Teverton went on.

Alina did not answer, and he said:

"And what about you, Lady Langley? Are you feeling the Romance of Rome beginning to make your heart beat faster?"

"Perhaps that is . . . something that will . . . happen before I leave," Alina managed to say, "but for the moment I have . . . seen only a . . . small part of Rome, and there is so much . . . more I want to . . . discover."

"Of course," Lord Teverton agreed, "so I will keep that question for a later date."

As he spoke, Denise joined them.

She was looking so lovely that Alina felt it would be impossible for anyone not to be over-whelmed by her.

Lord Teverton, however, hurried them into the carriage.

They set off for the Borghese Palace.

The horses carried them along the streets which were just beginning to be lit up for the evening.

Alina thought this was a greater adventure than anything she had experienced so far.

She would see the most famous Palace in Rome with its fabulous collection of treasures about which her Father had often spoken.

She would meet some of the most important Italians.

It would be something she would remember when she went back to England.

Just for a moment she saw in her imagination her Drawing-Room at home with the marks on the walls from which the mirrors and pictures had been removed to be sold.

She could see the faded sofas and chairs and the mantelpiece from which all the pretty orna-ments had disappeared.

Then she forced the picture away from her mind.

To-night Cinderella was going to the Ball.

She was not a penniless young woman who would have to earn her own living somehow, who had no assets apart from a house she could not afford to keep up.

To play her part she must believe she really was the rich Lady Langley, owning diamonds and elegant gowns.

Even as she thought of it, she saw Lord Teverton's eyes looking at her piercingly, and she was afraid.

The horses pulled up outside the Borghese Palace.

They had to wait while several other guests ahead of them stepped out of their carriages.

There were flares so that they could see their way up a flight of steps covered with a red carpet.

As they moved into the vast Hall in which they were to be received, Alina felt as if her breath were taken away from her.

Never had she seen anything so beautiful as the ceiling rioting with angels and cupids and the walls decorated with a brilliance beyond what she had ever seen or imagined.

Then they were being greeted by the Prince and Princess Borghese.

The glorious background, the glittering jewels, the splendidly-liveried servants, were everything that a Fairy-Tale Princess could desire.

More guests were announced as they moved on, and a handsome dark-eyed young Italian held out his hand to Lord Teverton.

"How are you, My Lord?" he said. "It is good that you are in Rome again."

"I am delighted to be here, Your Highness," Lord Teverton replied.

The Italian then glanced towards Alina, and Lord Teverton said:

"Lady Langley, may I present His Highness Prince Alberto Borghese!"

Alina held out her hand.

To her surprise, the Italian Prince took it in both of his.

"I know now," he said, "that this evening is going to be a very important one, because I have met you!"

chapter five

The Dining-Room was beautiful.

Alina looked around the huge table which seated forty people.

She realised that the seating had been altered because she and Denise had joined the party.

As would be expected, the Dowager Countess was sitting on the right of their host.

Alina herself had been placed on his left.

At the other end of the table Lord Teverton was seated next to the Princess and the Earl was on her right.

Denise, of course, was seated next to him.

The party consisted of a number of what Alina thought must be the Dowager Countess's special friends, because they were mostly much older.

Prince Alberto, who was on her left, informed her that a number of people were coming in later.

"We had thought," he said, "as the party was for the Countess of Wescott, that we would have singers from the Opera. However, as my sister is young, she wanted to dance, and I thought the Earl, despite his impressive title, was young enough to want to do the same."

Alina laughed.

"I am sure either entertainment would be delightful," she said. "And your Palace is so beautiful that what one feels about it could be expressed only in music."

"I wish I were musician enough to express in that way what I feel about you," the Prince said.

For a moment she looked at him in surprise.

Then she realised that he was flirting with her.

He continued to do so all through dinner.

It was for her a new experience, but one she might have expected because she was pretending to be an older and sophisticated woman.

She could see that the Princess at the end of the table was behaving very intimately with Lord Teverton.

She was not certain, however, whether he was flirting with her, or she with him.

Denise and Henry had eyes only for each other, and were not interested in the rest of the party.

When Alina looked down the table, she saw, as Lord Teverton had warned her, that the Italian Ladies were very smart indeed.

They all seemed also to be pouting their lips and flashing their eyes at the men next to them.

"I suppose I should try to flirt," Alina said to herself, "but I have no idea how to start."

Instead, she found herself blushing and feeling shy at the compliments Prince Alberto showered upon her.

"You are lovely, exquisitely lovely!" he said. "Just like an English rose!"

"That is a symbol which everybody uses,"

Alina managed to say. "As an Italian, you should think of something more original."

She tried to sound crushing, as she thought a famous London Beauty would be.

But the Prince merely said:

"I have a number of very original things to say to you, but not here at this table."

However, as dinner progressed, he became even more daring.

Alina was eager to change the subject from herself.

She asked if the famous statue of Princess Pauline Borghese, which had been sculpted by Antonio Canova, was in the Palace.

"I will show it to you after dinner," the Prince replied.

"I have always heard it is one of the most alluring as well as one of the most famous statues in the world," Alina said.

"Her skin was like yours," the Prince commented, "and when she bathed in her house in Paris, a Negro servant carried her naked from her bath to her bed-room so that she could see the contrast between his skin and hers."

This was something Alina had not heard before.

But before she could say anything, the Prince said in a lower voice:

"I will carry you myself. I am sure the closeness if not the contrast between our skins will be very exciting!"

Because she could not meet the expression in

his eyes, Alina blushed and looked away.

Then she realised that from the other end of the table Lord Teverton was watching her.

She thought — although of course she could not be certain — that he was looking contemptuous.

When the elaborate and delicious meal was finished, the ladies and gentlemen all left the Dining-Room together.

They went into a very large and beautifully decorated room with exquisite pictures.

An Orchestra was already playing.

The Prince did not ask her to dance; he merely put his arms round her waist.

When she and Denise were doing lessons together, among their instructors they had an excellent dancing-teacher.

Alina had always longed to dance at a Ball.

However, by the time she was old enough to go to one, her Father had died and she was in mourning.

Now, she thought, it was thrilling to be dancing in such a marvellous Palace.

She was aware, too, that it was an exceptionally good orchestra, while to complete the story she was dancing with a handsome Prince.

The Prince was holding her a little too close.

Because she was engrossed in trying to make him keep his distance, she found it hard to listen to what he was saying.

"You are beautiful! Gorgeously beautiful!" he said as they moved round the room. "Even the pictures pale before your loveliness!"

Alina told herself he doubtless said this sort of thing to every woman with whom he danced.

She therefore did not reply, but looked round the room at the other guests.

She saw Lord Teverton was dancing with the Princess Borghese.

The Princess was looking up at him in what Alina thought was a very intimate manner.

She wondered if they were old friends and if he had ever made love to the Princess.

Then she was shocked at her own thoughts.

How could she think of such things?

Such thoughts had never occurred to her when she was living quietly at home in the Country.

"I must behave as Mama would expect me to behave," she told herself.

It was rather difficult with the Prince saying such intimate things in her ear.

She was relieved when the dance came to an end.

"Now I want to look at the pictures," she said firmly.

She moved across the room to where there was a very lovely picture of the Madonna and Child with St. John.

It was by Credi and she wanted to discuss it with Prince Alberto.

Instead, he said:

"That is one of my favourite pictures, and I know now why it has always attracted me."

"Why?" Alina asked unwarily.

"Because the Madonna has a slight resemblance to you," he said. "Only you in fact are more lovely than when Credi created her. Now I will always be dissatisfied with the picture because, although it reminds me of you, it is not you."

Alina could not think what to reply.

It was a relief when the Earl asked her for the next dance, and she accepted his invitation eagerly.

She thought he was being polite.

Then she realised that Denise was dancing with their host, Prince Borghese.

When they were moving round the floor he said:

"Denise has been telling me how kind you have been to her, and I am very grateful."

"It is delightful to have her with me," Alina said, remembering just in time that she was supposed to be not herself, but her Mother.

"Denise has also told me that Lord Teverton did not pay you much attention on the journey. In fact, that he travelled in his own compartment on the train to Dover, and in his own cabin crossing the Channel."

"I can understand it was tiresome to have two women thrust upon him," Alina said.

She felt she must somehow make excuses for Lord Teverton, as he had been kind enough to give her a hand-bag.

"According to Denise, he has a strangely cynical attitude towards women," the Earl went on.

"But my Grandmother informed me after you had been to luncheon at the Villa that he was crossed in love when he was very young. This perhaps may explain it."

Alina was interested.

"Crossed in love?" she asked. "What happened?"

"According to my Grandmother, there was a very beautiful girl whom Lord Teverton's Father and Mother were eager for him to marry. He genuinely fell in love with her despite the fact that he was being pressured in asking her to be his wife. But in proposing he made a terrible mistake."

"What do you mean by that?" Alina asked.

"She accepted him, but fortunately, just before the engagement was announced, he discovered the truth."

"And what was the truth?"

"She was marrying him entirely because he was rich, and her Father, who was a Nobleman, was heavily in debt."

The Earl paused.

Then as he swung her round to the music he added:

"As a matter of fact, the girl was already in love with somebody else."

Alina did not say anything.

She thought that now she could understand.

Lord Teverton's cynical and supercilious air where women were concerned was due to a woman having hurt him.

She was sure that because he was so good-looking, this had been a blow to his pride.

That would be another reason why he was autocratic, also why he was apparently unfeeling when he left a woman weeping.

However, she did not say anything of this to the Earl.

It was inevitable that a few seconds later he was talking about Denise.

She then danced with her host.

She thought he looked much older than his wife and was somewhat boring.

He danced badly, almost shuffling round the room.

He was obviously not enjoying the evening in the same way as everybody else.

She tried to talk to him about the pictures, but got little response, as when she spoke of the magnificent statues in the room.

She would have loved to know much more about them. Then she mentioned the garden.

Now there was a spark more interest in her partner's eyes than there had been previously.

Finally when she spoke of the Park, she learnt that he had recently installed deer and gazelles.

He was now considering having a private Zoo and importing wild animals like tigers and lions from overseas.

This was something Alina had not expected to find in Rome.

She thought it was another detail that she would remember with interest.

The dance ended and Prince Alberto was once more at her side.

"I have done my 'duty dances,' " he said, "and now I can enjoy myself with you."

Alina could hardly say that she had any "duty dances" to do.

She therefore danced again with Prince Alberto.

Then he said:

"I want to show you the garden."

"I have just been talking about it," Alina answered, "and I think it is a fascinating idea that he should import wild animals for the Park."

"I think it is quite unnecessary," Prince Alberto replied. "However, the garden is very beautiful, and I know you will enjoy it."

He led Alina out through one of the long windows.

She saw that quite a lot of the garden had been illuminated.

There were lights under the firs and cypress trees, and others lit up the statues.

The fountains were throwing their water iridescently into the air because there were lights hidden in the basins beneath them.

"How lovely!" Alina exclaimed, clasping her hands together.

"Very lovely!" the Prince echoed in a deep voice, but he was looking at her.

She went down some steps to look at one fountain more closely and found it was exquisitely sculptured.

The water was pouring out of a cornucopia held in the arms of a cupid.

"There is another one which is even more attractive farther on," Prince Alberto said.

They moved farther away from the house.

Alina was standing looking up at a very elaborate statue.

Suddenly she realised that the Prince was putting his arms around her.

"No . . . no . . . please!" she said quickly, trying to move away from him.

But he merely tightened his arm and asked:

"How can I stop myself when I find you irresistible!"

"I . . . I ought to . . . go back," Alina said in a frightened voice.

She was aware that they were much farther from the Palace than she had realised.

The boughs of the trees almost encompassed them.

"You excite me," the Prince said, "and I want to excite you. Are you really an icicle like so many other Englishwomen, or could I create a fire in your heart?"

"I . . . am an . . . icicle!" Alina answered quickly.

She was trying to escape from his arms.

But he was much taller than she was and, as she realised, very strong.

"I want you, Alina," he said in a deep voice, "and I will teach you about love — the love which is fiery, passionate, and Italian. It has nothing in common with the dull, milk-like emotion that an Englishman calls love."

His face was very near to hers, and she knew he intended to kiss her.

With a little cry she tried to thrust him away.

"No . . . no!" she exclaimed. "How can . . . you behave . . . like this when . . . we have . . . only just met?"

"I have known you for a million years," the Prince answered, "and I have searched for you ever since I have been a man. Now I have found you!"

His lips were against the softness of her cheek.

Alina gave a little scream.

He pulled her closer still.

She knew she was helpless and imprisoned by him, when a drawling voice said:

"I think, Lady Langley, that this is our dance!"

For a moment both Alina and the Prince were startled into immobility.

Then, as his arms slackened, Alina pulled herself free.

She ran toward Lord Teverton, who was standing just beside the cypress trees.

"I . . . I am . . . afraid I had . . . forgotten," she stammered.

"Then shall we go back to the Ball-Room?" Lord Teverton suggested.

"Y-yes — of . . . course."

She did not look at the Prince, who she knew was standing beside the statue.

She just walked ahead of Lord Teverton until they were clear of the trees.

Only when she thought they were out of ear-shot did she say in a small, hesitating voice:

"Thank you . . . thank . . . you! I was . . . frightened and did not know . . . what to . . . do."

"Surely you know that it is a mistake ever to go into a garden alone with a man?" Lord Teverton asked scathingly.

"I . . . I never . . . thought about it. I . . . I was . . . looking at the . . . fountains and . . . then —"

She paused.

It suddenly struck her that there was no reason for her to make excuses to Lord Teverton.

He did not speak.

They walked on until they came back to the Palace.

Instead of taking her in through the window by which she had left with the Prince, he took her to a side-door.

It had a portico.

As they stepped into it, they were in shadow.

Feeling nervous and upset, Alina waited for Lord Teverton to open the door.

Then unexpectedly he said:

"Try to behave with a little more propriety before we leave!"

He spoke scathingly.

Alina looked up at him, wondering what she should say.

He put his hand under her chin.

"If you are so hungry for kisses," he said, "why not seek them from someone of your own nationality?"

Before she could understand what he was saying, she felt his lips on hers.

She could not believe it was happening.

Then, while she was still bewildered, he opened the door.

He walked inside, leaving her standing in the portico.

It was a relief when half-an-hour later the Dowager Countess declared it was time she had to leave.

Denise and the Earl said they were ready to leave too.

Alina realised that they wanted the chance to be alone.

She drove back with them and the Dowager Countess.

But as soon as they reached the house, she went upstairs, leaving them in the Study together.

There had been no sign of Lord Teverton.

The Earl suggested it was quite unnecessary for them to wait for him.

"I will take you home, Grandmother," he had said to the Dowager Countess, "and then escort Denise and Lady Langley to where they are staying."

"Thank you, dear boy," the Dowager Countess answered.

When Alina reached her own room she stared at her reflection in the mirror.

It was as if she were seeing herself for the first time.

How was it possible that Lord Teverton, of all people, should have kissed her?

Then she knew that he was showing her in his own subtle manner how cheap she had made herself.

His kiss was really a punishment for bad behaviour.

It was not because she attracted him in any way.

It was the first time she had been kissed.

It was not the least what she had expected a kiss would be like.

His lips had been hard, and she knew it was because he was angry.

But why should he be angry with her?

She was no concern of his in any possible regard except, of course, as a chaperon for his Cousin in whom he was clearly not at all interested.

It was like a conundrum that kept whirling round in her head.

It always came back to the same point.

Lord Teverton had kissed her.

Although he had been angry, it was an experience which she felt she would not forget.

Now, as she thought about it, she realised she had at first been stunned into surprise.

Then, before he had taken his lips from hers, she had felt a little flicker within her breast.

It was like the water rioting from the fountain, a sensation she had never known before.

It was strange yet exciting, but she had felt it for only the passing of a second.

Then he had released her and walked into the Palace, leaving her alone outside.

"I think perhaps I have shocked him," she told herself.

She had no wish for him to despise her for the way she had behaved.

"Why does he not understand that I did not deliberately do it?" she asked her reflection.

Then she knew the answer.

Like the Prince, Lord Teverton assumed her to be a sophisticated woman of a sensible age, a woman who accepted the men who pursued her as her right.

"How can he be expected to know," she asked herself pathetically, "that I am only a stupid girl from the Country who has never been kissed before?"

Now she had been kissed.

Not by a man who was excited and attracted by her — but by Lord Teverton, who despised her!

Alina went to bed in tears.

It seemed foolish, and she was annoyed with herself for weeping.

But somehow the evening, which had started so gloriously, had ended in disaster.

She kept telling herself that there was nothing to be upset about.

It really did not matter one way or the other what Lord Teverton thought or did not think.

Yet all her thoughts came back to the same

point: he had left her on the doorstep.

It was as if she were something to be discarded.

When she reached the Ball-Room there had been no sign of him.

Then when with the Dowager Countess they had said good-night, the Princess was not there.

It might just be coincidence.

Yet, remembering how the Princess had looked at Lord Teverton during dinner, Alina could not help thinking they were together.

They were somewhere in her beautiful Palace.

The statues, the pictures, and the vast collection of treasures were, she thought, a perfect background for love.

She had not understood all the compliments Prince Alberto had paid her.

He must have been surprised, she thought, at the way she had behaved, like a School-girl rather than a woman, and certainly out of keeping with her appearance.

She was vividly conscious of the powder and rouge on her cheeks, and the colour of her lips.

She knew Denise was right.

It made her look not only older, but also like every other woman who was a social success.

In Lord Teverton's eyes she was simply one of the sophisticated Beauties who frequented Marlborough House in London.

'Underneath I am just a gauche *débutante* who does not know how to behave!' Alina thought bitterly.

Denise did not come in to say good-night to her.

Alina cried herself to sleep although she was not certain why she was doing so.

When morning came, Alina chided herself for being so absurd.

"You are in Rome. You have a chance of seeing everything that is beautiful, and yet you are making a fool of yourself!"

She also remembered that she had no reason to be concerned with Lord Teverton.

It was no business of his what she did or did not do.

"I am not a *débutante*, I am a widow, and I must not behave like a frightened, half-witted girl!"

When very late she went downstairs to breakfast, it was a relief to find there was nobody in the Breakfast-Room.

She was just finishing her coffee when Denise came in.

"What a wonderful, wonderful evening!" she cried. "Thank you, dearest Alina, for letting me be alone with Henry. He did not leave until two o'clock."

"Two o'clock?" Alina exclaimed. "What about Lord Teverton?"

"There was no sign of Cousin Marcus — thank goodness!" Denise replied. "I expect he was enjoying himself elsewhere, otherwise he would have been home earlier."

"Yes . . . I expect . . . he was," Alina said in a dull voice.

"Henry is calling for me at eleven o'clock," Denise said. "You will not mind, dearest, if we go alone, will you?"

"No, of course not," Alina answered, "but I hope nobody will be shocked."

"They will not see us," Denise said eagerly. "We are going to drive out of Rome to a place in the Country which Henry has discovered and where he says the food is delicious!"

She gave a little laugh.

"I only hope I can taste it, for actually I can think of nothing but him!"

"You do not . . . think," Alina asked a little nervously, "that your Cousin Marcus will consider it . . . wrong of . . . me to let . . . you go off . . . alone?"

"Henry thought of that, and when he comes he is going to say that he is taking me to see his Grandmother — that is, if Cousin Marcus is interested enough to ask the question."

Denise pushed her plate away before she went on:

"The best thing we can do is to avoid seeing him. I am going upstairs now to get ready. As soon as Henry arrives, I shall run down and jump into whatever vehicle he is driving, and we will be gone!"

Denise seemed to have everything organised.

Alina thought it would be a mistake for her to argue about it.

She merely hoped, because she disliked lying, that Lord Teverton would not ask her any questions.

Finally when she had finished her breakfast she went upstairs.

Denise, with her hat on, was ready and waiting for the Earl.

"Do not forget," she said, "there are a lot of things for you to see in Rome which you have not yet seen. And I have here, dearest Alina, some money, which I am sure you will need."

Reluctantly, but thinking it foolish to make a fuss, Alina accepted it from her.

"You are . . . so kind and . . . generous," she murmured.

"The kindness you have done me cannot be expressed in money, not if it were a million pounds," Denise answered, "and Henry is very grateful to you too."

She gave a little laugh before she added:

"Can you imagine what it would be like if I had one of my pompous, ultra-respectable relatives with me? She would be determined that we should speak to each other only when she was present!"

Alina laughed too.

"I am sure you are exaggerating."

"You do not know how stuffy they are," Denise said, "and Henry's Grandmother is very much the same. Whatever you do, do not go near her to-day, or she may ask you why you are not with me."

"I will keep out of her sight," Alina promised.

A servant came up to announce that the Earl was downstairs.

Denise gave a cry of delight.

Picking up her hand-bag, she ran down to him without even saying good-bye.

They drove away immediately.

Alina followed Denise down the stairs, and now she wondered what she could do.

There was so much in Rome that she wanted to see, but she had no idea where to begin.

There was a Guide-Book, she knew, in the Study which Denise had left there.

She went to the Study and found the book.

She was just going back upstairs, when Lord Teverton walked in.

If he had gone to bed late last night, he certainly did not show any sign of it this morning.

He was looking, she thought, very smart and extremely English.

"Good-morning, Lady Langley!" he said. "Where is my Cousin?"

There was a little pause before Alina forced herself to say:

"She has gone with the Earl to see the Dowager Countess."

"I saw them driving away," Lord Teverton remarked. "It was in the opposite direction — but no matter!"

'He would catch me out again!' Alina thought to herself.

Feeling it best to say nothing, she moved towards the door.

"What are you going to do with yourself today?" Lord Teverton enquired.

"I came here to fetch the Guide-Book," Alina answered.

"I had an idea," Lord Teverton said, "that one of the things you would want to see before you leave would be the Colosseum."

"Yes, of course."

"Well, as I have finished my business for the morning," Lord Teverton said, "let me take you there."

Alina looked at him in surprise.

"Do you . . . mean that?" she asked. "It would be an awful . . . nuisance for . . . you, and I am sure you have . . . been there a . . . thousand times!"

"Then this will be the thousandth-and-first!" Lord Teverton said. "Put on your hat and we will leave as soon as you are ready."

"I will be only a few minutes," Alina promised.

She went from the room.

The depression she had felt since getting up had vanished.

She suddenly felt Lord Teverton was not still angry with her.

He had actually offered to take her to see the Colosseum.

She had had no wish to go there alone.

It was wonderful that she could go with him.

Suddenly it struck her that perhaps he was apologising for the way he had behaved last night.

For a moment she was still.

Then she told herself that what was past was past.

What was the point of worrying about it?

"He is going to accompany me to the Colosseum!" she told her reflection in the mirror.

Then she was smiling.

And the sun was shining more brightly than she had ever known it to do.

chapter six

They walked into the Colosseum and stood in one of the Galleries.

Quietly Lord Teverton began to explain what it had been like when it was first built.

He described the scene very vividly with its huge crowd of more than fifty thousand spectators.

They were seated according to rank in the Galleries, with women allowed in the top Gallery only.

In the arena Gladiators fought one another to the death.

Men were pitted against wild beasts, beasts against other beasts.

It could even be flooded for mimic sea-battles.

All were spectacles to delight the blood-thirsty mob.

He described how the animals were hoisted up in cages from the dens below the arena.

He told her that whips had been found which had been used on them.

He made Alina shiver to think of the crowd becoming wildly excited by watching the cruelty and blood.

The smell of it intoxicated them as if it were wine.

The shrieks and cries from the Galleries were

even louder than those of the victims and the roar of the enraged animals.

She could not only see it all happening, but feel it.

Suddenly she felt overcome, as if the spectacle were actually taking place below her.

She must have looked very pale, because at once Lord Teverton stopped speaking.

Slipping her hand through his arm, he helped her down the steps to the exit.

His Chaise was waiting just outside.

He lifted her onto the seat, then sat beside her and picked up the reins.

They drove for a little way in silence.

Then Alina said in a low voice:

"I . . . I am . . . sorry."

"There is nothing to be sorry for," Lord Teverton replied. "It is what I felt myself the first time I visited the Colosseum."

She looked at him in surprise.

She had never imagined that he would feel as she had, that he would be upset by the thought of what both humans and animals had suffered there.

She wanted to ask him to tell her more, but for the moment she felt too weak.

She therefore said nothing.

They drove on until they came to a Restaurant.

"I thought we would have luncheon here," Lord Teverton said. "I found when I was here before it served the best fish in the whole of Rome."

Alina felt her weakness pass.

It was wonderful to think she would have luncheon with Lord Teverton.

Perhaps he would talk to her as interestingly as he had talked to her in the Colosseum.

The Restaurant was small.

The fish were displayed attractively so that a customer could choose what he wished to be cooked.

Lord Teverton did not ask Alina what was her preference.

He chose what he thought was the best.

Then they sat down in a comfortable corner seat with a window looking out onto a court-yard at the back.

In it were flowers and shrubs, and the sun was shining.

Alina found she had recovered completely from her weakness.

Lord Teverton, however, insisted that she drink a glass of golden wine.

When she obeyed him she said:

"It was . . . silly of . . . me to be upset . . . I hope you . . . you . . . will . . . forgive me."

"I am interested, perhaps the right word is 'curious,' to know why you felt just as I did," he replied. "I have taken quite a number of people, at one time or another, to see the Colosseum, but their reaction has been very different."

He then began to speak of other things, and he did not refer to the Colosseum again.

When they finished luncheon he drew his gold

watch from his waist-coat pocket.

"I must take you back," he said a little rue-fully. "I have an appointment with the King for which I must not be late."

"No . . . of course not."

Alina picked up the hand-bag he had given her and walked from the Restaurant.

She thanked the Proprietor for a delicious meal as he bowed them out into the street.

Lord Teverton drove the horses rather quicker than he had done during the morning.

When they arrived at the house, Alina said:

"Thank . . . you. Thank you . . . very much for being . . . so kind. I enjoyed . . . my luncheon . . . enormously."

Lord Teverton did not reply.

He merely smiled at her, lifted his hat, and drove on as if he were afraid of being late.

Alina went into the house, thinking it unlikely that Denise would be back.

There was no sign of her until five o'clock.

Then she rushed in excitedly to say that she had had a fascinating time with Henry.

He wanted to take her out to dinner.

"There is a place he knows where no-one will see us, and we can be together and talk," Denise said. "You do not mind, dearest?"

"No, of course not," Alina replied.

"I feel mean leaving you alone, but perhaps Cousin Marcus will be dining in."

"Do not worry about me," Alina said. "I have a number of books I want to read, and it would be a mistake to let your Cousin know that I am not with you."

"Yes, of course," Denise agreed. "I am sure he would think it reprehensible that Henry and I want to be alone."

Alina therefore went to her bed-room.

Settling herself on the sofa, she opened one of the books she had brought upstairs from the Study.

She thought when Lord Teverton did return he would let her know if he was dining in.

Then she would have to pretend that Denise and Henry were dining with his Grandmother.

No-one came near her until, when it was nearly eight o'clock, there was a knock on her door.

"Come in," she said, and a footman appeared.

Speaking in Italian, he said:

"Milord is sending a carriage for Your Lady-ship at nine o'clock."

Alina's eyes widened with delight, and she jumped up from the sofa.

Lord Teverton was taking her out to dinner.

She supposed if he was sending a carriage for her, it meant he could not get away until the last minute.

Hastily she rang for the maid.

Instead of the Italian woman who had been looking after her, Denise's English lady's-maid answered the bell.

"I am going out to dinner with His Lord-ship," Alina said. "Please be very kind and help me with my hair and to choose a gown which I have not yet worn."

Jones, the maid, smiled.

"I'm glad Your Ladyship's going out," she said. "It's a waste being in Rome for you to sit here alone."

"That is what I thought," Alina agreed.

Jones ordered her bath to be brought in immediately.

While it was being prepared, they went to the wardrobe to decide which gown Alina should wear.

There was a very pretty one with lace draped over a full skirt of sky-blue satin.

It was not really elaborate enough for an older woman.

Alina thought, however, if she wore plenty of the jewellery that Denise had lent her, it would make her look older.

Jones dressed her hair in a particularly becoming manner.

Then she put on a necklace of turquoise and diamonds with large ear-rings to match.

Alina thought she would be very foolish if she did not know that she looked her best.

"Thank you so much!" she said to Jones.

"The gown's a little loose at the back," Jones said. "I'll just give it a stitch now, and if Your Ladyship'll ring for me when you get back, I'll undo it. To-morrow I'll sew on a hook and eye."

Alina thanked her again.

She picked up the wrap which went with the gown.

It was too hot to wear any of the capes that Denise had brought her.

Instead, she just had a scarf of the same material as the gown itself, but edged with lace.

"You looks beautiful, M'Lady!" Jones said with satisfaction.

A few minutes later a footman announced that the carriage was at the door.

Alina ran down the stairs excitedly.

She stepped into the closed carriage.

She thought as she did so that Lord Teverton was very lucky to be allowed to use his friend's stables as well as staying in his house.

The two horses drove off.

She wondered as they did so where Lord Teverton was taking her.

Would it be an even more delightful Restaurant than the one in which they had luncheon?

It was growing dark outside.

It was difficult to see much of the street through which they were passing.

Unexpectedly, they were no longer in a street.

Instead, they were moving between some trees.

Alina thought she must be in a Park.

Then the horses came to a standstill and there were lights.

She could not, however, see any large building, but there was a door ahead which was invitingly open.

She got out of the carriage.

Lord Teverton had certainly thought of somewhere original for them to have dinner.

As she walked in she could see ahead of her not a large room, as she had expected, but a terrace and beyond it the shimmering water of a lake.

A question came to her mind.

Even as it did so, a man stepped forward from between two pillars.

It was Prince Alberto.

Alina stared at him in sheer astonishment until he said:

"Welcome, my beautiful one! I cannot tell you how thrilled I am that you are here."

"Wh-where am I?" Alina asked. "I was asked out to dinner by Lord Teverton."

The Prince laughed.

"As I knew that His Lordship would be dining with His Majesty, I thought it would save a great deal of argument if I invited you to dine with me in his name."

Alina gasped.

"How could you do such a thing?" she demanded. "I think it very deceitful of you!"

"I adore you when you are angry!" he replied. "In fact, I adore you in whatever mood you are in."

He put out his hand.

"Come — our dinner is waiting, and we are both hungry."

Alina felt it was difficult to protest.

She knew now where she was.

She was in the little Temple of Aesculapius in the Borghese Park.

She had read about it and seen it from a distance.

She thought it was exquisite, but she had never imagined she would ever be actually inside it.

Now she was aware that a dinner-table had been laid for two on the terrace.

On a side-table there were a number of dishes set out attractively.

There was no sign of any servants.

Alina realised she was alone with the Prince.

She felt very nervous.

At the same time, she was sensible enough to know that if she tried to run away from him, he could easily prevent her from doing so.

Moreover, it would be impossible for her to find her way home through the Park.

"I must behave as the sophisticated lady I am pretending to be," she told herself.

She took off her gloves and sat down at the table.

It was decorated with several exquisite pieces of gold craftsmanship.

There was also a profusion of white orchids.

The Prince placed a dish of *pâté* in front of her before he sat on the opposite side of the table.

"I want to look at you," he said. "I have dreamt of how we could be together like this and I could tell you how beautiful you are!"

"I would much rather you told me about the Temple," Alina said. "It is very fine and I am wondering when it was built."

"In 1787," the Prince replied. "Now tell me

when you were born."

Alina found it difficult to keep the conversation from herself.

The Prince asked her questions and paid her compliments.

As he did so, he looked at her with burning dark eyes which made her feel embarrassed.

She found it difficult to know what she was eating.

She was careful to drink very little.

She was aware that whenever she took a sip from her glass he filled it up again.

As they ate, the stars came out overhead.

A full moon shone over the lake, turning the water to silver.

It was very romantic.

But Alina kept wishing she was not with the Prince and that he would not be so effusive.

He was certainly very good-looking.

Yet for some reason she could not explain he did not attract her in any way.

His exaggerated compliments made her feel uncomfortable.

She was afraid to meet his eyes because of the expression in them.

When they had finished what she thought must be the last course, she said:

"I must not be late in going back. Denise is dining with the Dowager Countess, and she will expect me to be waiting for her when she returns."

The Prince laughed.

"They may deceive you," he said, "but I am quite certain that Henry and your little *protégée* are dining somewhere secretly together and are as happy to be alone as we are."

"I am not at all happy to be alone with Your Highness," Alina retorted. "You brought me here by a trick, and I must insist that you send me back very shortly."

"How can you tell me to do anything so ridiculous?" the Prince asked.

He rose from the table and held out his hand.

"I want to show you what else the Temple contains."

Slowly, because she did not want to touch his hand, Alina rose.

She tried to avoid him.

However, the Prince took hold of her hand and drew her into the Temple.

There was a thin passage through which she had entered.

Then she was aware there were rooms on either side of it.

"This is what I want to show you," the Prince said.

He opened a door and she saw a small but beautifully decorated room.

There was a large divan at one end of it which was as big as a double-bed.

There was a window looking onto the Park at the other end.

The room was lit with candelabra in the shape of cupids, each holding three candles.

The air was fragrant with the scent of roses.

As Alina looked around her, she was aware that the Prince was taking off his evening-coat.

He flung it down on a chair as she said hastily:

"Thank you for showing me this pretty room, and now I must go!"

He walked towards her in his shirt-sleeves.

"Do you really think I will let you leave?" he asked. "My precious, my beautiful little Madonna, I have brought you here to teach you about love, of which, like all Englishwomen, you know very little. But after tonight it will be different."

Alina gave a little cry of horror.

He reached out his arms.

She ran away from him through the door he had left open back onto the terrace.

She looked first to one side, then to the other.

She realised in horror that the Temple was built out onto the lake.

There was no way on either side of the terrace by which she could reach the Park.

Because the Prince was aware of her predicament, he did not run after her.

He merely walked slowly until he was standing beside her.

"You are shy and elusive," he said, "and that, my sweet, excites me all the more! I want you — God knows I want you — and I intend to have you!"

He put out his arm, and Alina knew despairingly there was no way of escape.

He would carry her back to the room they had just left.

However much she might protest, he would make her his.

"Oh . . . God . . . save me," she prayed.

In that instant she knew the answer.

Taking the Prince by surprise, she moved away from him, not as he might have expected, either to one side or the other, but straight ahead into the lake.

The water rose first up to her knees, then nearly to her waist.

Lord Teverton, who had dined with the King and Queen, left the Palace as early as he could.

It was a privilege to be invited to what was an informal dinner.

At the same time, he found it somewhat heavy-going and had no wish to linger when the meal was finished.

He thanked Their Majesties profusely for their hospitality.

He accepted an invitation from the King to discuss further the proposals put by the Prime Minister.

To present them had been the reason for his coming to Rome.

Then with a sigh of relief he stepped into his carriage.

It was still comparatively early and he wondered if Alina had gone to bed.

He was still thinking that the way the Colosseum had upset her this morning was rather intriguing.

As he had said to her quite truthfully, it was how he had felt himself on his first visit.

He had been only twenty and a student at Oxford.

He had never known anybody else who had felt the same.

He thought there must be some rapport between himself and Lady Langley which he had not expected.

She was beautiful — that he recognised.

But there was something different about her beauty which he could not quite explain.

The carriage drew up outside the house and he walked into the Hall.

He waited for a footman to remove the evening-cloak from his shoulders.

Before he could do so, Jones, the lady's-maid who had accompanied his Cousin from London, appeared.

"But where's Her Ladyship, M'Lord?" she asked. "She hasn't come back with you?"

Lord Teverton stared at her.

"Come back with me?" he asked. "What are you talking about?"

"Her Ladyship said she was going to dinner with Your Lordship," Jones explained. "I'm waiting up so that I can help her undress."

"I am afraid you are mistaken," Lord Teverton replied. "I have been dining at the Palace with Their Majesties."

Jones stared at him.

"That's very strange, M'Lord! A message came for Her Ladyship to say you'd be sending a carriage for her at nine o'clock."

For a moment Lord Teverton was still.

Then he reacted quickly.

"Stop the carriage!" he said sharply to the footman who was standing nearest to the door.

The horses were just being driven away.

The footman quickly ran out, shouting to the coachman, who heard him and pulled them to a standstill.

Lord Teverton looked at the other footmen.

"Who took the message to Her Ladyship?" he asked.

Lord Teverton spoke extremely fluent Italian.

One of the footmen who spoke no English replied:

"I did, Milord."

"And who brought it?" Lord Teverton asked.

"A man. He were wearing livery, Milord."

"Did you recognise whose livery it was?"

The man thought for a moment.

"I think, now Your Lordship mentions it, 'twas the livery of the Prince Borghese."

Lord Teverton did not wait to hear any more.

He ran down the steps and climbed into the carriage.

As he did so he gave the coachman instructions as to where he wanted to go.

At dinner he had listened to an attractive woman who was seated on his left.

She told him scandalous tales of what was going on in Rome.

"It is Prince Alberto," she had said, "who keeps us all on tenter-hooks as to what he will do next. He is a very naughty boy, but, of course, we enjoy his endless *affaires de coeur*. He keeps us all guessing as to who is to share with him his next *amore*."

Lord Teverton had not been particularly interested.

He thought the Prince a somewhat tiresome young man, but his dinner-partner continued:

"His Highness takes whoever he fancies to the small Greek Temple in the Borghese Park. He has made an alluring bed-room at the back of the Temple and keeps the whole of Rome guessing as to who will be its next occupant!"

She had laughed.

The gentleman on her other side had confirmed what she said, adding a few anecdotes of his own to which Lord Teverton had listened.

He knew now who had spirited Alina away in his absence and where she would be.

He was angry, extremely angry, at the impertinence of it.

At the same time, his cool, calculating mind was thinking shrewdly.

It would be a mistake to let this become a Diplomatic incident.

There was always the possibility that it could disrupt the mission he was carrying out on behalf of the Prime Minister.

Standing up to her waist in water, Alina was afraid to go any farther.

If the bottom of the lake sloped down any lower, she would be out of her depth.

She could swim, but not very well.

She thought that nothing could be more humiliating than to have the Prince rescue her from drowning.

Astonished by what she had done, he was standing on the edge of the terrace.

She knew he was wondering what he should do.

"Come back, Alina!" he said finally. "You have made yourself wet for no reason whatsoever, and I will dry you to prevent you from catching cold."

Alina did not answer.

She was trying to think of some way by which she could avoid retracing her steps.

But she felt despairingly that sooner or later that was what she would have to do.

Then, as she felt her body sinking a little lower into the water, she moved nervously.

At that moment she heard a drawling voice say:

"Good-evening, Your Highness. As I was passing, I thought I would give Lady Langley a lift home."

The Prince, utterly astonished, turned.

Lord Teverton was standing just behind him.

For the moment he was so taken aback at his

unexpected appearance that he could think of nothing to say.

Lord Teverton walked forward to the edge of the terrace.

Then he looked with an expression of surprise at Alina, standing in the lake.

"It is a warm night, Lady Langley," he drawled, "but I think it would be a mistake for you to linger in your present position for too long."

With a feeling of irrepressible relief Alina began to move back slowly.

Her skirt, clinging to her legs in the water, was impeding her embarrassingly.

The Prince swore a lewd oath beneath his breath and walked away.

When Alina reached the place where Lord Teverton was standing, he put out both his hands.

He had to pull her up beside him.

The water was pouring off her satin and lace skirt.

She bent down to try to squeeze some of it from the folds.

Without saying anything, Lord Teverton removed his evening-cape and put it over her shoulders.

Having done so, he drew her from the front of the Temple and down the passage.

The door was open and his carriage was outside.

"I will make the carriage very wet," Alina said in a whisper.

"It is of no importance," Lord Teverton answered.

He helped her onto the back seat.

Then he went round to the other side of the carriage and got in beside her.

Her hands were clasped together, her wet skirt making a pool of water on the floor.

As they drove off, Alina whispered:

"I . . . I thought I was being taken to dine with y-you."

"I learned that when I returned to the house," Lord Teverton replied.

"Thank . . . God you . . . c-came . . . I was so . . . frightened . . . very . . . frightened. There was . . . no other way I could . . . escape . . . from h-him."

The words tumbled out of her mouth almost incoherently.

"Forget him!" Lord Teverton said. "And it would be a great mistake for you to talk about what occurred to-night."

"O-of course . . . I would not . . . talk about it! How . . . can you . . . think I . . . would?"

She tried to speak defensively.

At the same time, she was very near to tears.

Lord Teverton did not reply, and they drove on in silence.

It was only a short distance to the house, and when they arrived Lord Teverton said:

"Go straight upstairs, and if your maid asks questions, simply say it was an accident."

He was speaking sharply, as if he were addressing a naughty School-boy.

As Alina went up the stairs to her room, she

thought miserably that he must despise her.

And he must be ashamed of her too for being so foolish.

Jones was horrified by the state of her gown as she helped her out of it.

"Never mind, M'Lady," she said, "I'll hang it somewhere to dry, and when I press it, I'm sure it'll look as good as new."

Alina thanked her and got into bed.

In the darkness she thought how lucky she was that Lord Teverton had come at exactly the right moment.

She was sure that otherwise she would have been unable to escape from the Prince.

He would have done what he intended, no matter how much she pleaded or protested.

"Lord Teverton saved me!" she whispered.

She knew that only he could have been clever enough to find her.

Only he could have carried off the whole incident so diplomatically.

The Prince had not raged at him or, worse still, challenged him to a duel.

Duels were still fought in Italy, as they were occasionally, if secretly, in London.

'I am sure to-morrow His Lordship will be very angry with me,' she thought.

Then she knew she could not bear it if he were.

She did not want him to despise her for her stupidity, but to admire her.

She was suddenly very still.

Incredible though it seemed, she was in love!

In love with Lord Teverton, who was finding her nothing but a nuisance!

"I love . . . him! I love . . . him!" she said in the darkness.

She felt a little quiver in her breast. Then she realised the same thing had happened when his lips had touched hers.

chapter seven

Alina awoke with a start.

Somebody was shaking her shoulder.

She opened her eyes and saw that it was Denise.

"What is it?" she asked.

She felt as if she had been asleep for only a few minutes, although actually it had been several hours.

"I am sorry to wake you, dearest," Denise said, "but we have to leave for England almost immediately."

Alina gave a little gasp and sat up in bed.

"Wh-what has . . . happened?" she asked.

"When Henry got back last night to his Grand-mother's," Denise exclaimed, "he found a cable from England to say that his sister, who is older than he is and a widow, is desperately ill."

"I am . . . sorry," Alina said.

"He came here at eight o'clock to tell me," Denise went on, "and I went downstairs to talk to him. He is now arranging with Cousin Marcus for us to travel back in his private railway carriage."

"And we . . . are going . . . at once?" Alina asked in a small voice.

"You have a little over an hour before we leave the house," Denise said. "As soon as Jones has finished my packing, she will attend to yours, but I think you should start on it at once."

"Yes . . . of course," Alina agreed.

Denise went from the room, and Alina got out of bed.

She walked to the window, looking out over the roofs of Rome.

So this was the end.

She had been in this enchanting City for such a very short while.

Now the fairy-story was finished and she would go back to England to be herself again.

She felt as if there were a hard stone in her breast.

She knew that the real reason for her unhappiness was not that she was leaving Rome, but, rather, Lord Teverton.

She was aware that he would not come home with them.

He had not finished the work he had come here to do.

That meant that she would never see him again.

While she was thinking what this would mean, two Italian maids came hurrying into the room.

They brought with them one of her trunks.

Alina quickly dressed herself.

By the time she went downstairs for breakfast, the maids had practically emptied the wardrobe and the drawers.

There were only a few more things left to pack in the last trunk.

There was nobody in the Breakfast-Room.

When a servant brought in a fresh pot of coffee, Alina could not help asking:

"Has His Lordship had breakfast?"

"His Lordship has gone out, Milady."

Alina knew her last hope had vanished.

When the Earl arrived, he confirmed it.

"I am very sorry, Lady Langley, that we have had to do everything in such a hurry, but I am sure you will understand that I must go home immediately, as my sister is so ill."

"Of course you must," Alina agreed.

"She has been under the care of the doctor for some time," the Earl went on, "but they do not seem to know what is wrong with her. I only hope it is nothing really serious."

Alina gave a little murmur of sympathy.

Before she could say anything, he went on:

"I know you will understand that I will be able to cope with everything once I am back in England, even if it means an operation."

He paused for a moment, then added:

"Oh, and by the way, Lord Teverton asked me to say how sorry he is that he could not say goodbye to you. He had a very important meeting with His Majesty, which, of course, he could not ask to be postponed."

"I understand," Alina said.

She went upstairs and tipped the maids who had done her packing.

Then she collected the warm cloak she had worn on the outward journey.

When she came down again, the carriage was outside.

The Courier who had escorted them to Italy was attending to the luggage.

They drove off, all three of them sitting on the back-seat of the carriage.

Denise was holding the Earl's hands to comfort him.

It was a great achievement that at such short notice Lord Teverton's Drawing-Room carriage had been attached to the Express.

It was because, Denise explained, her Cousin ranked as an Ambassador for England.

He could therefore get things done quickly.

They boarded the train.

Alina remembered how Lord Teverton had travelled with them so reluctantly on the journey out.

He had made it quite clear from the very beginning that he had no wish for their company.

Yet he had been so kind to her once they were in Rome.

She would never forget how yesterday he had taken her to the Colosseum and afterwards they had luncheon together.

Then in the evening he had taken the trouble to save her from Prince Alberto.

Perhaps, therefore, if nothing else, he felt friendly towards her.

Then, like a blow from a dagger piercing her heart, she understood.

He still thought of her as an older woman, not

as the unfledged girl she really was.

If he ever guessed at the truth, he would never want to see her again.

It was most unlikely anyway that he would take the trouble to do so.

One thing was absolutely certain.

She had seen how he behaved towards Denise and knew he had no time for girls.

The wheels of the train as they rumbled under her were saying over and over again:

"It is finished . . . finished . . . finished . . . finished . . ."

Lord Teverton had arranged that they should have hampers of food as they had on the journey from England.

But the Chef in Rome had very little time to prepare them.

The food was therefore not as inviting as it had been before.

The Earl's Valet waited on them and was very attentive.

Somehow, however, everything to Alina seemed different and flat.

She was glad she was tired and had an excuse for going to bed early.

She left Denise talking to the Earl in the Drawing-Room.

She was, however, still awake when Denise came to bed.

Denise undressed, then said to Alina in a low voice:

"There is something I have to say to you, dearest."

"What is it?" Alina asked, also speaking very softly.

She guessed that Denise did not want the Earl to hear what they were saying from his sleeping-compartment.

"You do understand," Denise whispered, "that when we reach London you must go home immediately?"

"Yes, of course . . . I know that," Alina agreed.

"I have no wish for Henry to learn or to guess I have lied to him about you," Denise said. "Although he has forgiven me for the way I behaved with Charles, he has not forgotten it. I must not do anything which seems to him underhand or unconventional."

"I understand that," Alina agreed, "and as soon as we reach London, I will go straight home."

"What we have been deciding," Denise went on, "is that if Henry's sister is dangerously ill, we will be married quickly, before she dies."

She paused before she added:

"You will understand better than anyone that I could not bear to have to wait until the six-month period of mourning is over before I could marry Henry."

"I think it is wise of you to marry him at once," Alina replied, "even if it will have to be a very quiet wedding."

"That is what we have decided," Denise said.

"But what I mind more than anything else is that you cannot be present at the wedding."

"I will . . . pray for your happiness . . . wherever I am," Alina promised.

"I am hoping that later, perhaps in a year or so," Denise went on, "I can tell Henry that your Mother is dead, and how much you mean to me, having shared our lessons together. Then, of course, we can see each other again and he will not be suspicious of you, even if you resemble your Mother so closely."

"I think you have thought it all out very sensibly," Alina said.

"I know I seem to be behaving very selfishly," Denise went on, "but I suspect, although I am so happy with Henry, that he is still a little doubtful of my love. So I must be very careful."

"Do not worry," Alina replied. "I will disappear, and when we do meet again he will not have the slightest idea that I am anything but a young girl . . . a year younger . . . than you."

Denise gave a little laugh.

"It was clever of me to think of having you with me," she said. "You have been perfectly wonderful! I know that if it had been anybody else who chaperoned me, they would not have allowed me to be alone with Henry as I had to be in order to convince him that I really do love him."

"And now you will live happily ever after!" Alina said. "I do think you would be wise to marry as quickly as possible."

"I shall see to that," Denise said, "and, dearest Alina, I can never thank you enough."

She put out her hand towards the other bed and laid it on Alina's.

"What I am going to do," she said, "is to send you all the clothes I have now when I buy my trousseau. I have also written you a cheque for two-hundred pounds, which I slipped into your hand-bag when I was undressing."

"It is . . . too much!" Alina protested. "I cannot . . . take it!"

"Do not be silly," Denise replied. "You have to live, and I cannot bear to think of you trying to earn money in some servile or mean occupation. The two-hundred will keep you comfortable until we can be together in the future."

"But, I . . ." Alina began.

"Do not argue!" Denise interrupted. "It will only upset me and make me worried about you even on my honeymoon. You could not be so unkind as to make me do that!"

"Thank you, darling, thank you!" Alina said.

Denise had been so kind to her that she felt she wanted to cry.

She knew this was not her only reason for tears.

They were fortunate in that they did not have to change trains at Paris.

After a long stop they set off again for Calais.

By the time they reached London they were all very tired.

The Earl was on edge because he was worried about his sister.

He was also afraid, Alina suspected, that she might already have died, in which case it would be impossible for him to marry Denise for some months.

He had telegraphed ahead and carriages were waiting for them.

The coachman was able to tell him that his sister was alive.

The carriage for Alina took her directly to Paddington Station.

The Courier had ascertained that there was a train to the station nearest to her village.

She could catch it with only a three-quarters-of-an-hour's wait.

On the Earl's instructions the Courier went with her.

She sat in the Waiting-Room until he escorted her to the platform where the train was waiting with a Reserved Carriage for her.

She thought it was an extravagance she could not really afford.

But she learnt that either the Earl or Denise had paid for everything.

All she had to do was to thank the Courier, which she did most profusely.

He said good-bye and walked away, having also tipped the Porter.

'Denise has been so kind, so very kind!' Alina thought as the train left the Station.

Then once again she felt she was being carried

farther and farther away from Lord Teverton.

She suspected that by now he was enjoying having the house in Rome to himself.

He could spend his time with the beautiful Princess Borghese or somebody like her.

Alina had not forgotten he had told her how *chic* Italian women were.

If he admired them, there was no doubt that they would admire him.

"I must be sensible," she told herself. "It was an adventure which I shall always remember, but it is no longer part of my life and I have to live without it from now on."

What she was really thinking was that she would have to live without Marcus Teverton.

However sensible she tried to be about it, the agony was there in her heart.

Her love seemed to grow as swiftly as the train carried her out of his life and back into her own.

It was the fifth day since she had come home.

Alina came in from the garden carrying a bunch of roses.

She had already filled several vases in the Drawing-Room, and there were red roses in a large bowl in the Hall.

There had been a great deal to do when she had first returned home.

First she had unpacked her trunks.

Then she called on the Vicar to thank him for looking after the house.

She had gone round inspecting everything.

Staying in the beautiful mansion at the top of the Spanish Steps had made her aware of how shabby her own home had become.

She was therefore determined, without being extravagant, to make it as beautiful as she could, even without the many things she had sold.

She cleaned the walls until the marks where the mirrors and pictures had been were no longer visible.

She washed the covers of the chairs and sofas.

They certainly looked brighter and more attractive.

She was now determined to darn the patches where they were threadbare.

Mrs. Baker had helped her to clean the carpets so that she felt they looked almost like new.

This was an exaggeration.

The whole room, however, did look very much better, and the flowers made up for the absence of the china ornaments.

She put the roses down on the table by the window.

As she arranged them in the bowl she had left there, she was wondering why she was taking so much trouble.

Who was to see the improvements she had made except herself?

Then she knew that in some strange way it was her love for a man she would never see again which was making her fastidious, not only about her home, but about herself.

She and Lord Teverton had shared an identical experience in the Colosseum.

If he did think of her sometimes, she wanted him to admire her.

She did not want him to think of her as the rather untidy, gauche girl which she actually was.

She wanted him to remember her as the elegant, exquisitely dressed woman whom he had said was beautiful.

There had been a genuine admiration in his eyes before he had taken her to dine at the Borghese Palace.

That was how she wanted him to think of her for ever.

It might be childish!

It might be just creating dreams that could never come true!

She vowed she would never again allow herself to become dowdy and despondent.

This morning she had put on one of the pretty gowns which Denise had given to her.

She felt it made her look very young.

It was of white muslin with little touches of blue ribbon threaded through the *broderie anglaise* with which it was trimmed.

There was a blue sash round her small waist.

It had a bow at the back which was like a bustle.

She had arranged her hair in the same attractive manner as Jones had done for Denise.

When she looked at herself in the mirror, she had thought it was becoming.

She finished the arrangement of the roses in the bowl.

In her mind they were a symbol of the beauty she found in Rome.

She wished she could offer them as a gift to the man she loved.

Her task finished, she went to the window. Should she go out again into the garden, or stay in the house?

Suddenly, as if she were dreaming, she heard a voice behind her drawl:

"The door was open, and as no-one answered the bell, I came in!"

For a split second she thought that what she was hearing was only in her mind.

It was one of the stories she told herself.

Then she turned her head.

Although it seemed incredible, he was there — standing just inside the Drawing-Room door and looking at her.

It was impossible to move, impossible to breathe.

He walked forward, and she knew that he was real.

She was not just seeing him in her dreams.

At last, as he reached her, Alina found her voice.

"W-what . . . has happened?" she asked. "W-why . . . are you . . . h-here?"

She thought there was a faint smile on Lord Teverton's lips as he replied:

"I wished to apologise for having been unable

to say good-bye to Lady Langley before she left Rome, but I had some difficulty in finding her."

Alina's eyes seemed to fill her whole face as she murmured:

"Y-you . . . wanted to find . . . her?"

"Naturally I wanted to find her!" Lord Teverton replied. "But when I asked my Cousin Denise where she was, she was very evasive in her replies."

He paused.

Because Alina felt his eyes were looking at her in a penetrating manner, she looked away from him.

There was a short silence before Lord Teverton said:

"Wescott was equally uninformative. Then I thought of asking Denise's father, who proved far more helpful."

Alina felt as if she were still holding her breath.

It was impossible to think coherently.

It flashed through her mind that Lord Teverton did not think she was her Mother.

He believed her to be who she was in actual fact — her Mother's daughter.

"Rupert Sedgwick," Lord Teverton continued, "was kind enough to tell me where Lady Langley lived, and I therefore made the journey to Little Benbury."

There was another silence before he added:

"What I learnt when I entered the village was that Lady Langley was dead."

Alina clasped her fingers together.

He was obviously waiting for an answer, and after a moment she said:

"Y-yes . . . Mama is . . . dead."

"I also learnt," he went on, "that the Funeral took place a month ago."

So he knew the truth.

Alina looked up at him pleadingly.

"Forgive me," she said, "please . . . forgive me . . . but Denise desperately wanted to go to . . . Rome with a chaperon who would not prevent her from . . . being alone with the Earl and especially . . . she did not . . . wish him to think . . . that she was . . . following . . . him."

"So you pretended to be your Mother in order to act as her chaperon!" Lord Teverton exclaimed.

"It may have been very . . . wrong of me," Alina said unhappily, "but . . . Denise is very happy now . . . and there was no reason why anyone . . . especially you . . . should guess that I was . . . not who I . . . pretended . . . to be."

"Why — especially me?" Lord Teverton enquired.

"Because . . . you would have been . . . shocked and might have . . . told the family," Alina answered.

She gave a little cry and begged:

"Oh, please . . . you will not speak of what has . . . happened to . . . anyone? Denise does not . . . want the Earl or her Father or any of her . . . relatives to know. They . . . would be . . . very angry."

"And quite rightly," Lord Teverton said. "How could you have thought that someone as young as you would be a sufficient chaperon?"

"I am sorry . . . I have said I am sorry," Alina said. "Unless, however, you talk . . . nobody will . . . ever know."

"But *I* know!"

"You have found out," Alina said, "but, please . . . I beg you . . . keep the . . . secret!"

He did not answer, and after a moment she said:

"Oh, why did you have to come here and . . . discover the truth? I cannot . . . believe it was . . . just because you . . . had not said . . . good-bye to me . . . in Rome!"

"No," he agreed. "There was another reason."

She looked at him enquiringly.

She was thinking as she did so how handsome he was and how smart.

Because he was standing so near to her, her heart was beating tumultuously.

She was afraid he must hear it.

'I love him! I love him!' she thought. 'But he must . . . never have the . . . slightest suspicion that . . . that is how I feel!'

She was waiting for the answer to her question.

When he did not speak, she asked again:

"W-what . . . was the . . . reason?"

She thought somehow it was important.

To her surprise, Lord Teverton moved a step closer to her.

"I had to know," he said very quietly, "whether your lips were really as soft and pure and innocent as they seemed when I kissed you."

Alina stared at him in astonishment.

Before she could move, his arms went round her.

"I have come a long way to learn the truth," he said.

Then his lips were on hers, and she felt as though the whole world had come to an end.

He kissed her and now his lips were not hard, but gentle.

As her body seemed to melt into his, his kiss became more demanding, more possessive.

Alina felt that he drew her heart from between her lips and made it his.

The love they felt for each other seemed to envelop them.

It was as if the sun had come into the room and surrounded them with its dazzling light.

Lord Teverton raised his head.

"Now, tell me," he said, "what you feel about me."

"I . . . I love you," Alina whispered. "I . . . cannot help it . . . but I love you . . . and I thought I would . . . never see you again."

As she spoke, her eyes filled with tears.

"And I love you!" he said, and his voice was very deep. "But how could you have done anything so outrageous as to pretend you were a sophisticated woman rather than a girl who had never been kissed?"

"Did I seem . . . so very . . . inexperienced?" Alina whispered.

"I kissed you because you were so beautiful," Lord Teverton said. "But I thought that like all other women, you were flirting outrageously with every man you met, and were perhaps just pretending to be afraid of the advances that Prince Alberto was making to you."

"How could . . . you think . . . such things about . . . me!" Alina asked.

She knew the answer without his having to say it.

She was painted and rouged.

She looked like the sophisticated Beauties with whom he spent his time in London.

There was a little pause.

"Yes, that is the answer — until I kissed you! Is it true that you had never been kissed before?"

"Nobody has . . . ever kissed me . . . except . . . you," Alina said.

There was a little catch in her breath.

Now several tears had run from her eyes onto her cheeks.

He pulled her close to him and kissed them away.

Then his lips were again on hers.

He held her captive and made her feel as if she were flying in the sky and her feet were no longer on the ground.

She was breathless as he asked in an unsteady, deep voice:

"How can you do this to me?"

"Do . . . what?" she whispered.

"Make me feel as I believed I would never feel about any woman. It means, my darling, that I am very much in love!"

"Is . . . that true?" Alina asked. "Can it be . . . true? How can . . . you love . . . me?"

Lord Teverton smiled.

"Very easily, and I promise you, my precious, that if we feel as we do now, this is only the beginning."

He saw the question in her eyes, and said:

"I am asking you, my darling, how soon you will marry me?"

Alina felt her heart turn a dozen somersaults before she managed to say:

"Are you . . . are you really . . . asking me to . . . be your wife?"

"As quickly as possible," Lord Teverton replied.

He thought as he spoke that he had never seen a woman look more radiant, so exquisitely happy, or so beautiful.

Then Alina gave a little gasp.

"But . . . how can we be married?" she asked. "If I . . . marry you, it will be the most . . . wonderful . . . miraculous thing that has ever happened to me! But the Earl will then guess . . . the truth . . . and I could not . . . spoil Denise's happiness!"

"Denise or no Denise," Lord Teverton replied firmly, "I am going to marry you. We must just be as clever as you were, my lovely one, and think out an explanation of which nobody will be suspicious."

"But . . . you were . . . suspicious!" Alina pointed out.

"I was suspicious only after I kissed you," Lord Teverton replied, "and I assure you, nobody is ever going to kiss you in the future except me. Prince Alberto was very lucky that I did not kill him the other night — or at least throw him into the lake!"

Unexpectedly Lord Teverton laughed.

"Only you, my darling, could think of anything so surprising as to walk into the lake to save yourself from the amorous advances of the Prince!"

"I . . . I was frightened . . . and I could . . . find no . . . other way of . . . escape."

"I realised that," Lord Teverton said, "and it was very clever of you. But it is something which will not happen again because I will never let you out of my sight. You are far too beautiful — far too alluring — not to be *properly* chaperoned, and that is the right word."

Alina moved a little closer to him.

"Do you . . . really think . . . that I would . . . want anybody to kiss me . . . except you?" she asked. "I thought the Prince was . . . repulsive! Of course I . . . realise now that . . . I thought of him . . . like that because . . . I was already . . . in love."

"Not half as much as I intend you to be in the future," Lord Teverton replied.

Alina rested her cheek against his shoulder.

"Is it true . . . really true . . . that you . . . love

me? I felt as I came . . . away from Rome that . . . every minute was . . . taking me farther and farther . . . away from you . . . until you were . . . completely out of . . . reach."

"I came to England determined to see you the moment I arrived," Lord Teverton said. "When Denise was so vague about your whereabouts, I began to be terrified in case I could never find you again."

"But . . . suppose . . . when we are . . . married you are . . . disappointed in me?" Alina asked. "After all, I am . . . only a g-girl . . . and you . . . you hate . . . girls!"

Lord Teverton moved his lips over the softness of her skin.

"That is something you will not be for very much longer!"

"But . . . how can we be . . . married without . . . hurting Denise?"

"I have been thinking about that, and it is really quite easy," Lord Teverton replied. "You are resident in this Parish and your Vicar will marry us secretly to-morrow morning."

Alina gave a little start, but she did not speak and he went on:

"We will then leave immediately for my yacht which is at Folkestone Harbour."

His lips moved nearer to hers as he went on:

"We are going to have a very long honeymoon, my darling. I will teach you about love and it will be the most exciting thing I have ever done in my life!"

Alina waited for his kiss, but he continued:

"As soon as we have left England, your Mother's death will be announced. Then three or four months from now, or whenever we are ready to come home, we will announce our marriage."

He smiled reassuringly before he went on:

"There is no reason why anybody, not even Wescott, should suspect that my Cousin Denise's friend with whom she had lessons and who is now my wife, has pretended to be anything but herself."

"You are so clever," Alina said, "and it will be like . . . Heaven to be with you . . . wherever . . . we go."

"That is exactly what I was thinking," Lord Teverton said. "We think alike, we feel alike, and, my darling, I know now you will be mine for eternity."

"That . . . is what I want you to say . . . and to think. Because I love you . . . I love you and there are . . . no other words in which I can tell you what I feel."

She saw the happiness in his eyes.

Then he was kissing her wildly, possessively, and now very passionately.

She felt that every nerve in her body responded to him.

He created a fire within her that was part of the fire she could feel on his lips.

It was so exciting, so rapturous, that she knew they had both found real love.

It was the love that she and Denise had talked about when they were young.

It was the love that is part of the Divine, the love that she had wished for at the Trevi Fountain.

The Fountain had granted her wish, and God had answered her prayers.

"Thank You, thank You!" she said in her heart.

Then, as Lord Teverton's kisses carried her high into the sky, she knew they were reaching out towards the Gates of Heaven.

Ro